THE HOT YEAR

The Hot Year was a wartime year; it was also the year in Lucy Slade's life which took her from St. John's Wood to Delhi and Rangoon and back again, changed and a little chastened, but at heart wiser and gladder than when she had set out. It seemed like two hundred years, so much had happened: marrying Miles Spender and meeting Steve McMahon, to begin with, and the endless predicaments in which Lucy's impulsive, scatter-brained nature landed her in India that was still British, and the continual round of parties with the Forces, which it was Lucy's patriotic duty to attend.

THE HOT YEAR

The Hot Year

by

Anne Piper

Magna Large Print Books
Long Preston, North Yorkshire,
BD23 4ND, England.

British Library Cataloguing in Publication Data.

Piper, Anne
　　　The hot year.

　　　A catalogue record of this book is
　　　available from the British Library

　　　ISBN　978-0-7505-3660-8

First published in Great Britain in 1955 by
William Heinemann Ltd.

Copyright © Anne Piper 1955

Cover illustration © Birgit Tyrell by arrangement with
Arcangel Images

The moral right of the author has been asserted

Published in Large Print 2013 by arrangement with
Anne Piper, care of Watson, Little Ltd.

Magna Large Print is an imprint of Library Magna Books Ltd.

Printed and bound in Great Britain by
T.J. (International) Ltd., Cornwall, PL28 8RW

Remembering the brave Wasbies (Women's Auxiliary Services Burma) who supported the Forgotten Fourteenth Army through months of jungle fighting and the even braver men who fought that nasty campaign wearing the Crossed Keys of 2 Div. from York.

PART I

India

Chapter One

As she had volunteered for North Africa, Lucy Slade was not surprised when the Ministry offered to send her to India.

'You surely never said you'd go?' Priscilla asked, chasing sausages round the frying-pan, in the basement kitchen in St. John's Wood.

'I was brought up in India,' Henry said. 'It's all right for a child, I loved it.' He leant more comfortably against the dresser and rested his head among the cups.

'Oh, Henry,' Priscilla said, irritated, 'do *do* something. Lay the table, or something; Lucy isn't a child, she's obviously outgrown the snake-charmer stage and think of the awful *mem-sahibs* and bridge-parties and calling on the brigadier's wife.'

'Not in the middle of a global war – that sort of life must be finished,' Lucy suggested mildly.

Henry began to potter about looking for the mustard.

'If I was in the Army,' he told them, 'I should be waited on hand and foot by obedient, doe-eyed A.T.S. I don't think any of you realise how important my back-room

13

investigations are. In any case, I rather fancy I hear a flying-bomb coming.' He stopped and crawled under the kitchen table. 'You can pass my supper down when it's ready,' he added, folding in his long legs with difficulty, 'and, Lucy, dear child, on the dresser I have left a Top Secret file which I could be getting on with.'

Lucy handed him the file and began to lay the table.

'It would be free government travel,' she pointed out.

'I remember,' Henry droned through the table-cloth, 'the white palaces of Rajputana lapped by stagnant, lily-covered lakes.'

'The office would be in Delhi.'

'And the six (or is it seven?) splendid dead cities of Delhi lying under the juniper trees in the stark and sweltering plain.'

'They say the government hostel is a new and comfortable building with every protection against heat.'

'I rode out in a carriage beside my father on a white horse.'

'They say I should need a bicycle as the office is three miles from the hostel.'

'Don't go, Lucy, we should miss you and it sounds horribly humdrum. Where is Rachel tonight?'

'Savoy, I think,' Priscilla said. 'Or it may be the Ritz. That doctor, Miles Spender, is on leave.'

14

'May we hope for a quiet evening, then?'

The house belonged to Rachel. Rachel was beautiful, generous and vague. She asked people to meals, to stay, to live. They were all her parasites, but being regular parasites were inclined to resent the sudden intrusion of newcomers Rachel had just met. Particularly if Rachel had forgotten about them and gone out.

'I rather think,' Priscilla said, 'that she asked that coloured gentleman to come round tonight with his oboe – or maybe it was tomorrow.'

'Oh, no,' Henry groaned, 'I refuse to accompany him again – he plays excellently, but he's so energetic. I'll go out to the pub.'

'What about the bombs?' asked Priscilla maliciously, handing down his plate of sausages.

'There is a table in the pub too.'

'Yes, but they wouldn't be so indulgent to your weaknesses as we are. Either they'd laugh or insist on sharing your shelter.'

'Plenty of room for you both under here too.'

'I can't hear anything, anyway,' Lucy said. 'If it was one it's down over Croydon by now.'

The bell rang.

Henry shot out from under the table.

'All God's chillun got wings,' he muttered. 'I'm off.'

'Don't be so *mean,* Henry. What shall we do with him?'

'He's come to see Rachel – not me.'

'But if you go, he won't even be able to play the oboe. Oh, Henry, please – I made some treacle tart,' Priscilla pleaded.

Henry turned back from the door reluctantly.

'I wish I wasn't so greedy,' he sighed, sitting down beside them at the table.

The bell rang again. Priscilla took off her apron and went upstairs to the front door. There were voices above in the hall.

'What about your intended?' Henry asked Lucy with his mouth full.

'What intended?'

'I rather fancied you and Colin had reached an understanding. What will he say if you dash off to the Far East?'

'I don't care what Colin says – he's not my guardian.' She considered with annoyance the possibility of Colin, who worked with Henry and was tonight out fire-watching, imagining he had any rights over her.

'I thought perhaps you might be in love with him?'

'Nobody ever said anything about it.'

'Well, I happen to know he's in love with you.'

'Why on earth didn't he mention it then?'

They were interrupted by Priscilla being scrupulously polite to the nervous West

Indian airman as she showed him into the kitchen.

'I'm so sorry,' they heard her say, 'that Rachel had to go out unexpectedly. I hope she'll be back soon – meanwhile do come in and have some coffee with us.'

He was uncertain and disappointed, but he did his best. Henry paid handsomely for his two large slices of treacle tart and later suggested they should go up to the drawing-room and try out the oboe.

It was a soft delicious June evening. Henry opened the french windows and they began to play.

Priscilla collected a mixed bag of socks, and sitting on the step into the garden to catch the last light poised her darning mush-room. Lucy settled on the divan in the corner to consider the advantages of free travel for broadening the mind, the terrors of submarines and snakes set against those of flying-bombs, and the possibility of marry-ing Colin and retiring quietly to Hertford-shire to raise a family and be out of it all.

She was almost asleep when Miles sat down beside her.

'Pretty new crown,' she said, touching his shoulder. 'You're back early.'

Rachel was over by the piano making the oboe feel at home. She looked particularly good in a startling cherry-coloured dress. Lucy felt, as always when Rachel came into

17

a room, half-alive and recovering from a long illness.

Miles stared at Rachel. 'Who is this bloody wog?' he whispered. 'Rachel remembered him in the middle of dinner and we had to come straight home.' His big shoulders were hunched up crossly.

'Don't be so blimpish, he's charming and an airman.'

'I can see he's an airman. What's he got to do with Rachel though?'

'Do calm down. Nothing. She doesn't go out with him, he only comes here from time to time to play Mozart in the most innocent fashion.'

'I don't like it.'

Miles was scowling like a small boy.

'I was going to ask her to marry me to-night. I'm posted overseas.'

It was tough going in Normandy then, at the end of June – Lucy's heart gave two twists, one for a marriage, two for a death, but she made her voice sound calm and impersonal.

'You still can ask her – the oboe won't stay late.'

'I don't want to now – you come dancing with me, instead.'

He turned round to look at her properly for the first time that evening. She laid her head back on the cushions and pretended to yawn, his eyes hurt her. She did not want to love him.

'Sorry, I'm too tired. I don't feel up to standing in for Rachel at this eleventh hour. Be good and listen to the music quietly.'

No question of marrying Colin if the idea of dancing with Miles turned her dizzy. She shut her eyes and summoned the stagnant lakes of Rajputana to blot out Miles's angry, vivid face.

'I'm going anyway,' he said. She opened her eyes again to see him standing up. 'Good-bye, Lucy. Be a good girl – let's make a date for my next leave.'

'By all means,' her voice was bright. 'I shall look forward to that.'

Rachel did not even notice he had gone till the end of the movement.

'Oh, really, he is so ridiculously melodramatic,' she said. 'I know he hates music, but half an hour wouldn't have hurt him. Did he leave any address, Lucy?'

'I don't think he knew it yet.'

'Oh well, never mind. I don't write letters anyway. He's sure, to turn up on his next leave.'

Sure to. And I can't bear any more of it, Lucy thought. I shall go to India to run away from Miles, and to hell with snakes and submarines.

Rachel and Henry walked the oboe down to his bus stop and did not return.

'Went to the pub I expect,' Priscilla said,

19

washing up. 'Have you decided?'

'Decided what?'

Lucy clattered four dry knives back into the drawer.

'About India.'

'Oh, yes. I'll go. It'll be a nice change.'

'I dare say it'll turn out much the same, going to an office every day, only on a bicycle and far too hot.'

'Don't you ever get restless and want something different to happen?'

'No. I only want less to happen and Allan to be shore-based.'

'Loving the right man must have a steadying effect.'

'Not actually steadying, but an urgent wish for the ship to stop rocking under your feet.'

'I suppose I only want my ship to rock faster and faster till I'm out of breath and no time to think.'

'Poor Colin.' Priscilla shook out the dish mop.

'That's more or less what Henry said – but I'm not Colin's keeper – he hasn't even asked me to be.'

'He's too shy, you snap at him.'

'He's so hangdog – he just moons around looking hopelessly ineffectual.'

'It's only because he's in love.'

'All I can say is I find it most unattractive.'

'I wonder,' Priscilla said, changing the subject and opening the door to the bunks in the back basement, 'how many of us will want to sleep down here tonight?'

Lucy joined her in the doorway. 'Henry, anyway,' she said. 'He won't be induced to go upstairs, any more than Rachel will come down. Can it be true that she really doesn't hear them? Every single one goes through me and out the other end. I think I really want to go East to get a good night's sleep.'

'Four bunks should do, then,' Priscilla reckoned. 'If any other coward turns up on leave in the night he can bring down his own mattress.'

The faces round the breakfast table in Rachel's house were often quite different from those at supper-time. On the whole the supper people were the regulars, working in London and living in the house, but at breakfast appeared other people who had blown in on leave, Rachel's innumerable cousins, brothers, friends who looked on the house as a temporary home.

Lucy was woken in the middle of the night by a noise that was not a bomb. She located Priscilla's gentle snores from the bunk below. Then she heard a crash and muffled swearing.

'Henry,' she whispered, 'I think there's a burglar.'

'Bother,' came Henry's voice, 'I thought you were both asleep.'

'What *are* you doing?' Now her eyes were

used to the dark she could see Henry in the doorway to the kitchen.

'Trying to move the table.'

'For heaven's sake – why?'

'I'm getting cramp sitting under it, not to mention the draught, and I had an idea I might fix it *over* my bunk. But it's heavier than I thought.'

She climbed down across Priscilla.

'Here – I'll give you a hand. Do you think it's wide enough?'

'I think so.'

Together they heaved the table into position as a canopy to his bunk.

'Do you think you'll learn to be any braver, Henry, as they go on?'

'I very much doubt it, though I hope to avoid any additional complexes by giving free rein to my fear.'

'What you will get,' she remarked, pulling her way up into her own bunk again, 'is claustrophobia.'

Henry poked his head out like a tortoise in the two-foot gap between his pillow and the top of the table.

'I'm afraid you may well be right,' he said mournfully. 'Or perhaps agoraphobia – what prospects do peace hold for me if I am forced to live in a tub?'

'Do you think it will ever be peace?'

'Speaking as one who planned and initiated the whole Continental invasion – I

22

believe it will be peace sooner than you think. Whether,' he added, and then paused to count as the distant drone came nearer and nearer, cut out, and came down, 'we shall live to see it is another matter. That one wasn't further away than Baker Street, I fancy.'

Priscilla, Rachel, Colin and Henry came to Euston to see Lucy off. The train steamed away to the safety of Liverpool just after a warning of Imminent Danger overhead had sounded. As the others waved, Lucy saw poor Henry's green face turn miserably to the glass roof of the station. A few minutes later she found a key to Rachel's house at the bottom of her bag. She would have to post it back some time. Good-bye, bombs. Good-bye, Europe. Good-bye, Miles, who had not written to Rachel and was probably dead around Caen by now.

For the first week of the long sea voyage, Lucy wandered about the ship alone, stunned and stupid, until Michèle, the small French girl with whom she shared a cabin, spoke to her sharply.

'You aren't pulling your weight, dear.'

Lucy looked up from a book at Michele brushing her dyed hair at midnight.

'Meaning what?' she asked.

'There are two hundred men on this ship.'

'Two hundred and six, the purser said.'

23

'One hundred and three for you, and one hundred and three for me.'

'You can have my extra three,' Lucy said generously.

'No – do be serious – I can't manage to entertain the lot, you must help.'

'Do they have to be entertained?'

'They seem to think so.'

'Perhaps you could organise a whist drive.'

Michèle laughed, a dried-leaf cackle which did not alter her dead-pan face.

'You do have strange ideas, Lucy. Don't you like men?'

'Very much. But I happen to be nursing a broken heart.'

'Me too.'

'Nonsense – you look very contented.'

'Nevertheless, my heart is in little chips, which does not prevent me considering the poor boys. Let them, at least, give you drinks.'

'I don't see what good it is going to do the poor boys to share my gloom over a glass of ginger beer.'

'You mustn't ask for ginger beer, it is *far* more expensive than gin. How can you mend your heart if you don't speak to anyone?'

'I don't want it mended.'

But in the shiny holiday blue of the Mediterranean she made an effort to be pleasant to some of Michèle's friends. They were all eager to tell her about their charm-

24

ing wives. They were all very, very devoted to their wives, and to their darling children, photographed from every unsuitable angle with large feet and ears. She was rewarded by an evening in a Port Said night-club where twelve outsize Egyptian ladies waved tatty veils and sang American songs. She was pushed doggedly about a cool, marble dance floor for several hours. Back in the ship, aching with exhaustion, she discovered that Michèle intended to hold a party for ten in their cabin, and escaped forward on to the dark deck where she fell asleep uncomfortably with her head on a coil of rope.

When the man tripped over her numb ankles she woke again, groaning, and shielded her eyes against the beam of a torch.

'Oh, hullo,' he said, 'it's the little dark one. You all right? Passed out?'

'No and yes,' Lucy replied with dignity, 'I was just snatching a short rest.'

'You certainly don't sound squiffy.'

'Why should I sound squiffy on a pint of ginger beer?'

'Sorry, mixed you up, of course it's the little blonde who spends all day in the bar. What's the matter then?'

'Hurt my ankle.'

'Sprained it?'

'No, strained both by the feel of it – dancing.'

'What a wonderful time you girls have– '

'Would you enjoy walking about five miles on hard marble crushed up against a starched white pocket till you get a crick in the neck, listening to how much better everyone's wife can dance?'

'Is that how they waste their time?'

'That's how.'

'Poor girl – you must come dancing with me some day – or is it necessary to have a wife first?'

'Well, well, well,' the jovial voice of the assistant purser bore down on them out of the night. 'Why aren't you at the party, Lucy? Everyone's looking for you, having a wonderful time.'

'Good night,' said the first man, leaving them alone.

'Don't trust that type,' hissed the purser as he sat down beside Lucy on the rope.

'Why not?'

'Journalist – out for trouble – they make it when they can't find it. You're a nice simple kid – I don't think you know what it's like East of Suez.'

'I expect I'll soon find out.'

'Yes – that's what I'm afraid of – I've seen so many girls ruined by the East.'

'Physically or morally?'

'Both – all quite spoilt, lose their looks, but still have armies of boy friends, think they're Helen of Troy – till they come home again to

26

Wimbledon and crash, down to earth among the dirty crockery.'

'I shan't be like that – honestly.'

'You'll see, I'll give you a year – you won't know yourself – hope you didn't mind a bit of good advice?'

'No – no – not at all.'

'What about a kiss to prove no hard feelings?'

'If I have to kiss all the people who lecture me about my ruin just to soften their feelings, I shall be ruined quicker than anything,' she pointed out getting to her feet and leading him back to the party.

The Canal Zone was a hot baked brown, but in the Red Sea the August sky grew grey, the sun disappeared and left the sea a deep, oily green. It was too hot to move. Lucy lay in her cabin for five days trying to read Trollope to still the gnawing thoughts of Miles.

'I shall hate India,' Michèle, lying on the lower bunk, confided through the mattress.

'What will you do in Delhi?' Lucy asked leaving the dank, refreshing pastures of Barsetshire.

'Drink, I suppose.'

'No – what sort of job are you going to?'

'Language broadcasts, being bilingual.'

She also had volunteered for North Africa.

'I suppose India can't really be worse than

a gas-fire in a bed-sitting-room near Victoria station,' she added in her flat voice.

'Perhaps you'll fall for James,' Lucy suggested. Michèle spent every evening in the bar with a tall naval officer. Michèle snorted.

'He already wants me to marry him and go up into the hills of Ceylon where he is to be a tea planter after the war. Can you imagine me on a tea plantation?'

'I believe all planters drink a lot, and not tea either, but I don't know about their wives. Perhaps they drink because they have no wives?'

'That would be good. I don't like women. They talk too much anyway.'

Thus rebuked, Lucy returned to Trollope.

Chapter Two

The ship docked at Bombay in pouring rain. The harbour officials wore, as they had in Liverpool, mackintoshes, but over the filth in the water buzzards floated lethargically to announce a strange hemisphere. The stucco buildings were peeling and shabby, the streets spotted with blood-red betel-nut juice.

They had to wait several days in Bombay for train reservations to Delhi. Outside the hotel in the evenings a peanut seller sat on the pavement with a small boy asleep beside him, singing from a book in the lamplight.

It rained and stopped and rained and stopped and clothes and hands were damp and sticky all the time. Lucy lay for hours of the afternoon hypnotised by the large, slowly moving fan in the ceiling. She could not remember the strength of the feelings which had driven her to India and was overwhelmed by a dreary grey dislike of all living. Why travel half round the world away from Miles when she could have crawled into the cotton mills in Manchester and been as soon lost?

Despair intensified during two days in the

Frontier Mail, rocking sootily northwards through mile after mile of featureless green plain. Sometimes a collection of mud hovels, sometimes a yellow river, very occasionally a near town with white and mud-coloured stucco buildings peeling. Once, at a station, monkeys in the trees, but no dignity, no splendid palaces, no mountain ranges. The only relief to the monotony the sudden sharper green of rice-fields. Michèle ate bananas and slept neatly without creasing her pleated skirt.

'You can wake me, Lucy, if you see an elephant.'

But she saw no elephant. At every stop the beggar children scrambled on to the train moaning for baksheesh; at first her heart was touched and she parted with a little money, but this led to such an ugly stamp-ede that charity quickly turned to fear.

'Don't be silly,' Michèle said without opening her eyes. 'Send them away or we'll be overrun.'

But they were banished by an Indian untouchable with a broom who leapt into the compartment and started brushing dust vigorously all over them until Michèle was forced to sit up saying: 'I don't believe this is part of the normal service.'

Between Agra and Delhi, as the day ended, the trees and the sky grew larger and Lucy saw a small boy tending a herd of black goats among the rocks, and later a peacock. Michèle changed her blouse and brushed her hair. Her friend, Irene, who had gone to India a year ago, should meet them.

'Though she probably won't know me. I was dark when she left.'

But Irene on the station platform screamed with excited recognition. She asked no questions about the journey, or England, but whisked straight into her battles with the hostel authorities for better conditions.

They sat late into the night in Irene's room to hear scandal about local villains. Outside the open window the crickets sang unceasingly and the Indian door-keeper cleared his throat with ghastly thoroughness.

When the party at last broke up, Lucy fell asleep with Irene's voice going on and on into her dreams:

'Whatever you do – don't have anything to do with Smith. He's murder.'

Apart from a frenzied determination to eschew Smith she woke with no clear idea about life in Delhi, and watched helplessly, while her bearer unpacked and put things away in unsuitable places. The room opened on to a balcony which ran the length of the squat concrete building. Beyond a line of trees a long straight road led nowhere in both directions. It was raining. She stood on the balcony staring cross-eyed at the road.

'Ah,' said Irene, breezing up behind, 'have

you got a bicycle yet?'

She had forgotten about a bicycle.

'But you *must* have a bicycle – it's the first essential – there's no other way to the office for a start. Ask your bearer.'

She had no umbrella either, so she stewed in a mackintosh as she rode over with Michêle in an expensive tonga to announce their arrival to the authorities.

In London they had understood that all sections were desperately overworked and understaffed in Delhi and their coming would be joyfully welcomed. They found nobody was even expecting them. After a good deal of file shifting it was indeed established that they were scheduled to appear, and that the authorities had themselves arranged hotel accommodation in Bombay. The authorities were pleased with that little bit of staffwork and pointed out several times that they had stayed in the best hotel.

'Yes,' they said patiently. 'But what now?'

Michêle refused to be placed in the accounts department, and finally forced them to admit there was a French section working down in the Radio building who *might* take her in. Michêle continued to be firm until they gave Lucy a note for the man in charge of the English news-room in the same building.

'Though I don't suppose,' the authorities

finished triumphantly, 'he has any room for you *there*.'

Before they took leave of the central office Michèle made sure they were both on the pay roll. It appeared there would be no difficulty whatever about *that*, and from now on they would be getting a large monthly cheque, come rain, come shine.

'Well,' Michèle remarked as they got back into the tonga, 'this is a funny old war and a half. Do you realise we had a destroyer escort all the way to Malta?'

Mr. McCleod in the news-room was horrified to see Lucy.

'Any news experience?'

'No.'

'Done any journalism at all?'

'No.'

A Reuter machine in the corner ticked on as ceaselessly as the crickets and gave a good impression of busyness.

'What on earth did they land you on me for?' he asked exasperated.

'*I* don't know,' she snapped – equally exasperated with six thousand miles of pointless travel. He softened slightly.

'Look here, we'll give you a try, but come back on Monday, there's a good girl – haven't got a spare chair today.'

The room was shaped like a half moon. She looked round to see faces of various colours bent over rough paper, at least everyone seemed to be scribbling – something must be going on. McCleod waved her off. She walked out into the rain. It was Thursday, about twelve noon. She drove back to the hostel to find a horrible old horse of a bicycle propped against the door of her room on the first floor. Her bearer appeared at once and together with a saintly old man in a turban, with a long beard (the owner of this superb machine), tried to persuade her that it was a three-speed racing model. She hoisted herself into the saddle and pointed out to them that she could not reach the pedals and that the brakes did not work. The old man told her it was a bargain and the saddle could easily be adjusted. She stepped down and waited to see an adjustment – together the bearer and the old man strained and banged; at first the saddle tilted to the right, then to the left, finally, thanks to the bearer's excessive enthusiasm, it fell off altogether. The old man, with a sob in his throat, at once accused the *memsahib* of wantonly breaking the bicycle, his only means of livelihood.

She was just wondering if she would have to pay him a pension for the rest of his days when a man stepped out of the room next door to hers and dealt with the situation very effectively. In three minutes her bearer had disappeared and the old man was staggering downstairs underneath the bicycle, wearing the saddle on his head and snuffling into his beard.

'Thank you so much,' she beamed at her benefactor, a tall, gaunt man with enormous glasses.

'A pleasure,' he replied. 'Come and have a drink.'

She accepted his gin gratefully and it wasn't till she was sitting down in his cane basket chair that he said: 'By the way, my name's Smith, Augustus Smith.' She nearly started up again remembering Irene's warnings and wondering how literally she had called him murder, but as the french windows were open on to the dripping balcony, she sat her gin out.

'And just what are you doing in this god-forsaken place?' he asked.

'Seeing the world,' she replied.

'You won't see it here – nothing but a squabbling, carping, hysterical, backbiting, second-rate selection of old England.'

'Thank you.'

'Oh, it takes a month or two to degenerate, you probably have ideas still, or ideals – it takes a few weeks to jettison the whole lot.'

'Have you been here long?'

'No, thank God – invalided out of China, went to pieces up there, but that was a country – something really going on – shan't be here much longer. Waiting for a home transfer.'

'London's not very restful at the moment,' but he ignored that; one was always done out of any chance to tell a bomb story. He shouted her down with the virtues of the Chinese.

'By the way,' he said suddenly, fixing her through his strong lenses, 'I'm collecting people's observations on how the heat affects them. I'm particularly interested in women's first reactions to it – how many clothes they wear – that sort of thing. If you like to type out a page or two for me, you needn't put your name to it – be treated in strictest confidence.'

She escaped saying she thought it was too soon to have any reactions, and found herself standing in the middle of her own room in floods of tears.

The official purpose of her transfer to another continent remained obscure. When, on Monday, she presented herself to Mr. McCleod he looked at her dazed, over his black beard, and said:

'Who are you?'

She reminded him that he had told her to come back then.

'What for?' he asked.

'You are going to teach me how to write a news bulletin.'

He looked round the room obviously waiting to use the 'no chair' excuse again, but there were two empty so he threw her a sheaf of Reuter strips and told her to read them. 'Read a few newspapers too,' he ordered.

For the first hour she read with nervous concentration, afraid that her presence would in some way hamper the news centre, until she noticed that the gentleman on her left, an elegant Sikh with a big turban and a very daintily rolled-in beard, was writing a letter.

McCleod roared his way out of the room for a conference, and the Sikh turned to her with a charming smile. 'How do you spell "retrograde"?' he asked. She had never seen such long eyelashes on anyone. With McCleod gone, everybody relaxed. The semi-dark gentleman on her right got out three tangerines and ate through them one after the other. He spat the pips on the floor and they were swept up with very little delay by a magnificent servant with a sash as well as a turban.

An altogether white gentleman at the far end of the room was reading a book on accountancy. The news machine ticked on, but nobody bothered to tear off the strips which coiled round and round on to the floor.

The semi-dark gentleman, Mr. Tamara, suddenly addressed her. 'I have very poor accommodation,' he said, spitting another pip. 'It is not correct that government officials have poor accommodation, and where am I to put my wife?'

Nobody answered.

'The question is,' he went on, 'shall I bring her here or not? What do you think? Do you consider this is a good job? They have said nothing about a pension.'

'I should leave your wife where she is,' said the Sikh without looking up from his letter. 'Who knows? The British can't last much longer, done for— '

She wondered if the defence of the British lay with her, but before she had made up her mind what to say she was relieved to see the man at the end abandon accountancy with a bang.

'Don't you believe it, Singh,' he said. 'Shan't go till we've shot all the Sikhs anyway – we needn't bother about you, the other side will shoot you as a traitor.'

'I'm not a traitor,' said the Sikh mildly. 'Would you put two "p's" in "repression"? I am a spy.'

The Englishman started to file his nails.

'You are a very lazy spy.'

'Not at all,' said Mr. Singh. 'I am writing very complicated code letters. I should have gone to Oxford if it were not for your silly war.'

'Is Mr. McCleod helpful to work under?' Lucy ventured, to change the subject.

'Excellent man,' said Mr. Singh warmly. 'A very excellent man.'

Mr. Tamara nodded his head. 'Most competent.'

'Of course they approve of him,' said the Englishman. 'He does all the work anyway, doesn't know how to delegate and wouldn't if he did. He works all the shifts – gets here at seven in the morning and leaves about eight at night.'

She contrived to get a little work to do by arriving for the early shift when McCleod was alone, disentangling the overnight news from the machine. At that time of day it was more than he could manage on his own, and he would let her bash out the current progress through the mud in Burma. Singh, Tamara and Gerard never came in before nine. That was indeed quite early enough to start writing letters and studying accountancy. She was soon writing letters herself well before lunch-time, and decided one morning that some sort of hay must be made before all will-power melted away.

'Mr. Singh,' she said, 'I want to see something of the real India.'

'Oh yes,' said Mr. Singh politely. 'Could you explain to me why this is a funny joke, please?'

She stared at the strip cartoon, and tried to explain.

'You see I am not wasting my time – I am

39

making a study of the British–' she interrupted him impatiently:

'How can I see India?'

'It is all round you.'

'I can't believe that Delhi is typical of India.'

'Plenty is going on here too.'

'But I see nothing.'

'You are not meant to see anything.'

'Please, couldn't you take me to Dusserah?' She had a very vague idea of the significance of this Hindu festival, but knew it involved fireworks.

'No. I cannot take you anywhere.'

'Why not?'

'My family would hear of it in the North and they would be horribly shocked. If my mother knew I had even spoken to a white woman she would faint away.'

'Why?'

'Because all white women are immoral, wicked and hideous. My sisters also could not speak to one.'

In the end they arrived at a compromise; McCleod, who had overheard the conversation, said he'd be the official escort if Singh would guide them both. Singh's guiding was not energetic. When he saw the size of the waiting crowd, about ten thousand, in an empty piece of ground on the outskirts of the town, he at first suggested driving straight back, but McCleod urged him forward.

'Come on, Singh. You lead – we'll make our way up to the front.'

Singh said Miss Slade would be the best leader, the people would be sure to make way for her, but she was relieved when McCleod strode ahead, pushing with a frankly top-dog firmness. She kept close to him while Singh strolled some way behind, looking in the other direction and pretending to have nothing to do with them.

The sun was just setting; before darkness came Rama, and his queen, Sita, drove round the ground in a chariot. As a climax he shot flaming arrows into vast effigies (about fifty feet high) of Raven, King of Lanka, and his two generals. The villains disintegrated in leaps of flame with starry rockets shooting from their vanquished bodies.

'Well now, Miss Slade,' Singh said politely as they were bouncing home in a tonga, 'you have seen India. Very soon she will go up in smoke and bangs just like that and you poor British will crumble away into a hot dust. Meanwhile you will do better to go dancing at the Gymkhana Club rather than concern yourself with us.'

'You can't mean that.' His bland smile infuriated her. 'It must be right that I should want to find out what is going on?'

'And what good will this vulgar curiosity do?'

41

'I could help somehow– '

'Help who?'

'Well, surely–' She appealed to McCleod, who was also smiling with irritating indulgence– 'every individual on either side who makes an effort to appreciate the situation must in some small way improve the chances of a friendly settlement–' She stopped, horrified at her pomposity, and tried again. 'I mean – if I make some Indian friends– '

'Impossible,' Singh interrupted. 'It is now quite impossible for any Indian with any self-respect to make friends with even an English man, let alone an English woman.'

'Singh's right,' McCleod said soothingly. 'It's gone beyond friendship now. You go dancing and raise the morale of the British Army – that's what you are here for really. Nothing so boring as a political woman. Just stop worrying about anything and you'll have a marvellous time out here. All the girls do.'

She concentrated fiercely for some weeks on enjoyment.

'My wife,' said the colonel, 'doesn't believe in bottling.'

'Really?'

'No, she says it takes all the goodness out of the fruit.'

'I expect it does really.'

'But do you know we've been married twenty years and I've never lost a garment through moth?'

'No – really?'

'Not one – of course, out here with only a damn fool of a bearer to look after my clothes, I've got moth all over my pants. Ada would have a fit if she were here.'

Just her luck, to draw the colonel who could not dance. Her eyes wandered enviously to Michèle, expressionless as usual, but spinning gracefully in the middle of the floor with the other colonel who, fifty if a day, was putting in some very neat footwork.

'My eldest daughter's over eighteen now.'

She expressed the expected astonishment.

'Can't decide whether to go into the Army or the Navy.'

'It must be very difficult.'

She pushed her foot, tapping impatiently, well back under her long skirt. Her whole face ached from the effort of not yawning.

'Wouldn't let any girl of mine come out here,' said the colonel sternly. 'Not fit for a woman now. When Ada was here in peacetime she stayed in the hills till well into October.'

'Fancy?' she said, but it sounded wrong, so she changed it to 'Really!' again. It did not make any difference, the colonel prattled on about his family till after midnight.

They took the girls home in a taxi, handing them out at the door with impeccable gallantry, assuring them that the evening had been a very good show and that they must do it again next time they came on leave.

'Michèle dear,' Lucy implored her, 'don't involve me with them in future; if they ask you, say your friend's feet have fallen off or something.'

That evening ought to have taught her not to join a party of Michèle's again, but she made one more terrible mistake before she realised that Michèle could not tell one human being from another, particularly if they wore trousers.

Michèle discovered that there was a stout French lady from Rouen running a hair-dressing establishment in the town and came back enthusiastic, with her head shining.

'You must go, Lucy. Have your hair all cut off and she'll give you a blonde rinse. It'll cheer you up.'

Lucy had reached a level of despair where some drastic physical change was essential. She had prickly heat under her hair at the back of her neck and a haunted feeling that she had lost her identity. Everyone she met seemed to be talking to themselves, or to the collective sympathetic ear of womankind.

She tried to fix herself in the looking-glass, but her face flickered and faded.

'Who are you?' she asked herself in a

hollow voice. She sat down and made a very short list of the people who might notice if she died of cholera. Not one of them was within four thousand miles. 'All right, Michèle,' she said grimly, 'I'll try it.'

Madame was a competent hairdresser. She snipped off the long black hair Lucy had grown laboriously, in about five minutes, then higher and higher, until, before there was time to complain, it was half an inch long all over her head and seemed to be twisting slightly.

'It was only the weight kept it down,' Madame said. She washed it, rinsed it, dyed it and dried it and Lucy came out of the shop puce in the face, her head covered with flaxen curls. While she was under the dryer, and in a weak and vulnerable state, Madame made her promise to come and see her at home the following Saturday. Michèle, she said, was already expected. Lucy had a vague idea of a cultured European evening. The French in India would not have been so affected by the Imperial atmosphere as the British. She agreed cheerfully.

Back with her looking-glass, she decided Madame had given the final death-blow to her identity. Friends and relations in England would hardly recognise her now. This time perhaps she really was beginning a new life.

'Do you think Madame will have invited

anyone else?' she asked Michèle as their tonga trotted down the long straight avenues to Madame's bungalow. Michèle was vague; she thought Madame might have said something about an American.

A servant showed them straight into the dark garden; it was a soft, cool night without mosquitoes. Several people were sitting in basket chairs drinking, it took some time to get used to the darkness and locate the little European dinner-party which consisted of three American colonels, one Irish group-captain, two pathetic Anglo-Indian girls, and a vivacious and tiresome Russian lady. Madame's husband turned out to be a melancholy, middle-aged Indian to whom she was not married. Lucy had had such a clear, preconceived picture of the evening that she did not realise at first that things were off-key. She sipped tomato juice, grateful for the darkness which meant that she need not even talk to her neighbour, and looked up at the velvet sky, feeling almost peaceful until she heard one of the American colonels end a long, and apparently point-less, story in a way which made her wonder if something had happened to her ears. A dutiful titter from the Anglo-Indian girls showed there was at least nothing the matter with her ears. They sat in the garden for another hour while the Americans and the Irishman capped each other's stories, and nobody else said anything, before Madame suggested a move indoors.

Another American, a major, had appeared. He sat down at the piano and began to play fast and noisy jazz. Madame, stout and dignified with ginger hair and a crimson *sari*, stood by him, idly stroking his head and directing the servants as they carried round refreshments. The group-captain and the Russian lady danced, shuffling ungracefully on the tiled floor. The Anglo-Indian girls drooped sadly over the piano as all the American colonels had fallen for Michèle now the light was on, but it was a mild orgy.

Three more people arrived, a Burmese girl escorted by two young British Army officers. One of them started to talk to Lucy and she found he had been at school with Miles. I will not talk about Miles, she told herself sternly, and continued to ask give-away questions about Miles as a small boy, a lumping, spotty, middle-sized boy, a tall, athletic, big boy.

'He was never very good at exams, was he?' she asked anxiously.

'Didn't have much time to work his last year. As far as I remember he was captain of everything, but he did scrape into the University. Do you know him well?'

'No, hardly at all.'

He looked a little surprised at her excessive interest, so she qualified it. 'I mean he's more or less engaged to a great friend of mine.'

'Look here. I hope you won't think this is awful cheek, but I really don't think you should be here. I'm sure Spender wouldn't like it.'

'I don't think he would mind either way, and anyway he must be dead in France – though I was rather wondering,' she admitted, 'how on earth I was going to get home.'

'Come on,' he said. 'Have you back in a jiff – got my jeep outside.'

On her way up the stairs she met Smith loitering. 'Come and have a glass of lime juice in my room,' he suggested. 'I drink a lot of it, find it a great help.'

She declined this tempting invitation.

Chapter Three

The peacock throne, the creamy marble of the Mogul palace, delighted her. The shining water slipped in imagination into the old dry channel which led from room to room.

'If there be happiness on earth,
It is here, it is here, it is here.'

the Mogul prince had engraved on his glowing wall. Had they trapped happiness, or for ever, like the poor Americans, pursued? If one waited here breathless, seeing the hanging gardens, the calm sky through fretted marble screens, would the dove descend?

She waited, hands clenched behind her back, prepared to receive eternity, but only heard a gardener outside grinding up for a good spit, while a beggar appeared at her elbow, whining.

On the way home she considered the beggar as a possible sign from heaven. Maybe happiness was lurking among the Indian poor. She saw herself staggering under basket-loads of roses, doing good works with an indomitable smile. She would not neglect the British either; in future she would go six nights a week, instead of one, to the Forces canteen. For an inbred Puritan, work not pleasure held perhaps the key to joy.

She met Michèle in the courtyard of the hostel as she came in.

'Nobody knifed you then?' Michèle asked.

'Oh no, why should they?'

She ran upstairs whistling, impatient to begin turning out the goods she intended to give to the poor. Her bearer padded after with her suitcases, he seemed anxious about something.

'*Mem-sahib* not cross?' he asked.

'No, *mem-sahib* gay as a bee.'

'*Sahib* said many times *mem-sahib* not cross.'

'That's right – *mem-sahib* happy, happy-going to lead a new life – the hart no longer pants.'

'Please?'

She pushed open the door of her room. Everything looked exactly as she had left it on Saturday, except that Miles was lying on her bed, asleep. She stood absolutely still staring at him, with the palms of her hands going clammy. He was clearly alive, ghosts don't snore, even a slight whiffle. Lord help me, she thought, I love him even with his mouth open. What am I to do?

'Thank you – you may go,' she said to the bearer, still staring at Miles.

'*Mem-sahib* not cross?'

50

'No – *mem-sahib* not cross.'

He went reluctantly. Miles was really too big for the narrow hostel bed, his feet hung over the end and one arm flopped down the side.

She knelt beside him, this time she would learn his face and remember it right. Large eyes, large nose, large mouth. In memory, with intensity of feeling, his face always dissolved, leaving nothing but his voice and his strong, gentle hands. She knew so little about his hands, only held or shaken a few times. I do not like him at all, he is arrogant, in love with Rachel, and a slight snorer – outside a bullock cart creaked down the road. She stretched out one finger to touch his hand and it closed round hers.

'Lucy,' he said, his eyes still shut.

'Hullo.'

'Good to see you.'

Oh yes, splendid – without even bothering to open your great big eyes.

'I thought you were dead, Miles.'

'Not dead, in Poona.'

'I was so sure it would be France.'

He blinked sleepily and then sat up, letting go of her hand.

'Blow me down. Shirley Temple, what *have* you been doing to yourself?'

She'd forgotten her wretched hair.

'It makes a nice change.'

'Who for?'

'Me, of course.'

'Well, I don't like it.' He lay down again.

'It wasn't done for you.'

'Whoever you fancy, he's no good if he advises that vulgar *coiffure*. Drop him at once and come out with me.'

'How did you know I was here? Are you on leave?'

'No, posted here to command the destruction of the Japanese – I got a letter from Priscilla just before I left Poona telling me you were here too.'

'How are they all?'

'Terrific – Rachel's just married Henry.'

'Oh, darling, I'm so sorry–'

Miles sat up and swung his legs round.

'Don't come the little mother over me.'

She tried to cover up the terrible warmth in her last remark.

'I only meant jolly bad luck old chap and better luck next time,' she said defensively.

'The hell you did – I won't have you being sorry for me. If she chooses to marry that spinster aunt, she's welcome, and good riddance to her, and you know perfectly well I never asked her to marry me, so what's it got to do with you if she doesn't?'

'Nothing, Miles, nothing – don't shout.'

'Why shouldn't I shout?'

'Because there's an awful man next door called Smith who works afternoon shifts, and will have his ear gummed to the wall anyway.'

'What kind of a place is this?'

'Lousy. Where are you billeted?'

'I haven't been there yet – came straight here off the night train – and where have you been in such secrecy the last two days? They told me you were due back today, but your address had been eaten by rats – showed me a torn piece of paper to prove it. Who were you with? This curl tweezer?'

'And what's that got to do with you. You can't come dashing back from the dead to pry into my private life. If I choose to go off for the week-end, I shall go off for the week-end.'

He took her wrist and pulled her towards him.

'Let go – or I shall scream.'

'Scream away – it's you who was worrying about Smith. Listen to me, I've always had a high opinion of you, Lucy, and I don't like to arrive here and find you've gone to the dogs already. You used to be such a good, quiet, reliable girl in London. Now, because we are old friends, are you going to tell me who you've been away with?'

'Why?'

'Just so I can go and have a fatherly chat with him – make sure his intentions are honourable, etc. I'd like to see you married to the right person.'

'Oh, you would, would you?'

'Yes, of course I would – marriage is a fine

institution, and a girl does herself no good to ignore it.'

'Any minute now, you'll be saying it's different for a man.'

He looked surprised.

'But of course it is.'

He gave her wrists an extra shake. She wrenched them free and stood up.

'You'd better get it into your head,' she said grimly, 'that we are *not* old friends, we never have been friends and I don't suppose we ever will be, and even if we were you wouldn't have any right to talk to me like that. Now will you go, please?'

'I thought perhaps I could sleep here to-day. I haven't got to report till this evening, and you'll be out at work, won't you? We could have dinner together–' He seemed to have understood nothing. He smiled at her comfortably and yawned.

'Look,' she said, resigned. 'Don't you realise that I don't want to see you?'

'You will by dinner-time.'

'I'm not free tonight.'

'Cancel your date.'

'Why should I?'

'Because I don't arrive every day of the week.'

'But you are going to live here – I dare say by Wednesday week I may find you less irritating and we might have lunch – but for the moment I never want to see you again.'

She was delighted to find how much she disliked him, stupid, overbearing man, and his hands far from gentle.

'Off you go to work, then,' Miles waved her away, 'then you won't have to see me till tonight.' He put his feet back on her counterpane.

She went out, banging the door, but stuck her head in again to say, 'You might at least take your boots off,' before giving the door a second slam.

She found no one had stolen her bicycle (an old gent's model bequeathed her by an officer leaving for Burma) in her absence and after the usual difficulty she had mastering the machine sufficiently to mount, she rode away down the long avenue to the office, her heart bumping with joyful clichés such as 'hulking brute', 'pompous idiot', 'self-satisfied ass of a rowing blue'. She was not at all sure that Miles was a rowing blue, but in her present mood she felt it to be likely.

McCleod looked surprised to see her.

'Thought you weren't coming back till Tuesday?'

'Changed my plans.' Change of heart – free, free, free. It was an effort not to sing to McCleod.

'Nothing for you to do,' he said.

'Really nothing?'

'Not a thing. You'd better beetle off.'

Up on the round roof of All India Radio there was a small canteen. She sat down at a table by the parapet and ordered breakfast. The eggs took ages to come, giving the normal impression that it had been necessary to light a wood fire and build up a good glow, besides inducing the hen to lay.

Over the edge of the parapet Lady Linlithgow's green trees stretched for miles in all directions, hiding all the blank, square, identical bungalows.

Ten avenues away Miles lay sleeping and she did not love him.

Captain Mortmain bicycled up behind her at noon as she was pedalling towards the shops.

'Hullo old girl.' He slapped her so heartily on the back that she nearly swerved under a taxi. 'How was Dusserah?'

'Oh, really–' she felt thoroughly cross, what with being nearly knocked down, too hot, and unable to go home and have a bath and change. 'What do you mean?'

'No good being cagey with me – the Intelligence learns all. Come and have lunch.'

'You know – seriously,' he remarked over his second drink, 'I envy you, Lucy. Do you know I've been twelve years in India now and I've never had a chance to speak to an educated Indian?'

There seemed no answer to this.

'In my job,' he went on, 'it simply wouldn't do.'

'Why not? The intelligent ones might give you more idea of what's going on.'

'Oh, we know what's going on all right, don't you worry about that.'

She hadn't worried.

'From now on we'll be keeping an eye on you.'

'And what good does that do you?'

'We know when and where trouble is likely to start.'

'What sort of trouble did you think I might start?'

'Don't know – but we'll be reading all your mail now, so watch your step, old thing.'

'Oh, honestly–' She rushed out of the hotel, angry and tearful, without waiting for her lunch.

A sharp little Scottish missionary called Miss Campbell shared her shift in the canteen that evening. During a lull in the bacon and eggs and chip orders she suddenly turned on Lucy.

'You're a spoilt lot, all you girls out here.'

'Oh, I don't know,' Lucy said feebly.

'Think about nothing but having a good time.'

'Depends what you call good.'

But she wouldn't be put off.

'Drinking, dancing – and trying to catch

the highest-ranking officer. Ever consider that a major may have been a dustman in peace-time?'

Lucy had not considered this.

'Look at all these nice boys here– '

Miss Campbell waved an arm at the humble privates and corporals downing chips. 'How many of them have taken an English girl out since they landed in India?'

Lucy really did not know.

'Aren't you ashamed?'

'But there are so many thousand – millions,' she pointed out helplessly. 'And none of them have asked me anyway.'

'Of course, they don't dare to ask,' Miss Campbell snorted. 'I think it's disgusting.'

'Perhaps they are all married.'

'Even if they are it would give the poor things fighting for you up in all that mud a little simple pleasure just to speak for a few minutes to a girl from home. Just selfish hussies, the lot of you.'

She wondered whether Miss Campbell herself went out with many corporals.

A few minutes later Miss Campbell called her over to the other end of the counter.

'Come here, Miss Slade,' she ordered, 'I'm sure you will be interested in the sergeant's photographs.'

The sergeant's wife was sweet and shy on the beach, trying to hold her hat on and her dress down in a strong wind. That was

58

before the war, the sergeant explained. His children, now six and seven, scowled at them furiously. They had never been to the seaside.

'You see?' said Miss Campbell to her cryptically. 'I hope, you are due for home soon, Sergeant?'

But the sergeant had left England last month and had never seen the mud of Burma.

'You see?' Lucy retorted, but Miss Campbell only put her head through the hatch into the kitchen to bellow: 'Ek chips,' to the cook and did not speak to her for the rest of the evening.

As she bicycled home in the darkness through the roaring of the cicadas she tried to shake off the day's attacks and recapture the morning's light-heartedness. She pedalled furiously and then free-wheeled. Just outside the hostel as she swerved out, the better to sweep in, she collided with an Indian who was dashing up in the opposite direction on the wrong side of the road and without lights. A jeep behind them braked noisily and several people, including the doorkeeper, began shouting. She picked herself up and tried to drag the twisted remains of her bicycle to safety, but found she could not walk. It felt as if she had broken her ankle. She sat down again on the pavement and waited for someone to take charge. The driver of the jeep was abusing the Indian cyclist, the Indian cyclist whined drearily, and the doorkeeper lamented over the lot of them.

The jeep backed to catch her in the headlights. She blinked stupidly at the man getting out.

'Don't think I touched you, did I?' he asked from far above her head.

'No, no, not at all,' she replied politely.

'Can you stand?'

'No – but it's quite comfortable here.' She put her elbows on her knees. The corpse of her bicycle seemed to have grown four wheels, embroidered with stars. 'Hey!' he said, as she slumped-sideways into darkness towards him. She came round a short time later to see real stars rushing above her head.

'Where are you taking me?'

He stopped the jeep and turned to her.

'Glad to hear you're with me again – I thought the hospital, not knowing your name and address. Are you strong enough now to tell me?'

She could not see his face but the voice was familiar.

'I don't know that I want to go back.'

'Lost your memory?' He offered her a cigarette and in the light of the match she saw a long thin face with astonishing eyes. The match burnt out before she had established a colour beyond brilliance. She did not answer, perhaps one could mislay memory with a strong enough will. Destroy this futile job, this doomed city, the long, long journey of escape that had only led round again in the hot, trampled snow to Miles.

'Do you believe in free will?' she asked. 'I make frequent decisions to lead new lives. I think I'm taking a definite step away from the tram-lines and they crowd up all round me like iron railings.'

'I'm sure this is no moment for decision – just relax and see if you can't remember at least your name.'

'What's yours?'

'Steve MacMahon.'

'I thought there was a bit of brogue in it.'

'I fight it down, but whispers of neutrality get through.'

'It's funny – I'm sure I know your voice.'

'I rather thought I knew your face. As a matter of fact I was following your bicycle because you looked like a girl I travelled out with, only she was dark.'

'That's me,' Lucy said. 'Last August. What are you doing in Delhi?'

'Misinterpreting your cause to Dublin – what are you?'

'That's a leading question.'

'Can't you even remember if it's an office? Or maybe you are a nurse, or the colonel's daughter – do try to think.'

'I'm thinking.'

I am an untrained, unsuccessful, unloved sub-editor. I wish I was dead, or at least in London with my feet up talking down the telephone to a friend no farther away than Flaxman. If I was in London I could write a kind letter to poor Miles in the Far East once a month. A patronising, pity-you-aren't-here, letter.

'Look,' Steve said, 'if you can't remember, I think we'd better push on to the hospital. You must be pretty bad.'

She began to laugh hysterically – not remember every single melancholy detail: the concrete floor, the Kashmir rug, the silver fish in the chest of drawers, the shrieking crickets, the boring, boring, boring men – and Miles. The dreary alternation of boredom and pain – painful boredom and boring pain. She rocked to and fro sobbing with laughter.

'Stop it.' Steve spoke sharply and she ended on a gulp of surprise. 'What's your name?'

'Lucy Slade.'

'Where do you live?'

She told him.

'But, good lord, that's where I picked you up.'

'Yes, I know. I was just turning in the gate when it all happened.'

'What a girl – getting a nice ride off me

under false pretences – and you in your right mind and right place all the time.'

'I'm sorry – I've been a nuisance. I really did black out for a while.'

He lit a match and looked at her face.

'It's my ankle you should be studying.'

'Does it hurt?'

'Like hell.'

'Like last time we met. My turn to apologise, back home and send for the doctor.'

He carried her across the gravel and up the hostel stairs. At the top they met the inevitable Smith.

'Oh, has there been an accident?' His eyes lit up. 'Let me help.'

'Call the doctor if you want to help,' Steve told him curtly, kicking open Lucy's door so that Smith got a good view of Miles comfortably reading in the basket chair.

'I'm *so* sorry to interrupt,' Smith said. 'I didn't know – I'll telephone at once.' He leered at them all and backed away like a conniving pander.

'Good-bye. I gather you'll be all right now.' Steve nodded towards Miles.

'Thank you.' Lucy balanced on the door-handle. 'I'm sorry if I made you late for anything.'

'Not at all, it was a pleasure – command me any time.'

'The one with glasses was Smith,' she remarked when Steve had gone, hopping over to her bed. 'So you'll be all round the hostel in the strictest confidence by break-fast time.' She tried to muster some anger through the pain. 'Anyway, I thought you had to sign in this evening?' Miles closed his book.

'I did. Just came back to make sure the sun didn't go down on our wrath.' He smiled at her benignly and stood up to go, saying: 'So that tall, thin gentleman is the one you went away with?'

'No, I didn't,' she said, 'he just picked me out of the gutter.'

'What gutter?'

'I fell off my bicycle – didn't you hear the crash about twenty minutes ago?'

'I did hear something, but wherever I go in India there is always a crisis with confused crashes and swearing, so I didn't pay much attention.'

'Well, that last crash was me.'

She shut her eyes as the pain streaked up her leg and opened them to find Miles bending over feeling her ankle.

'What do you think you are doing?' she asked roughly. His fingers were gentle, but any touch excruciating.

'Only a bad sprain – nothing broken.'

'Are you sure?'

'Yes. After all, I ought to know.'

'I thought even a doctor didn't know with-out an X-ray?'

'Trust me – you'll be on your feet again in a couple of days. What shall I use for a bandage?'

He opened the door of her cupboard. 'What a tidy girl – everything folded and in the right place.'

Dull, neat, reliable, unexciting Lucy.

She closed her eyes again, this time to keep back tears.

'Shall I tear this?' Miles asked, holding a lawn nightdress. She sat up, furious.

'No – for heaven's sake, no! Look, you go now. Smith has sent for a doctor anyway and I suppose he'll bring a bandage with him.'

Miles sat down again in the chair on the opposite side of the room.

'I'll just stay to make sure everything's all right.'

'Of course it'll be all right. If it's only a sprain what could go wrong?'

'The combination of Smith and an Indian doctor is not reassuring.'

'A qualified Indian doctor would be as good as an English doctor.'

'I beg to differ.'

'Oh, you're as exasperating as the rest of them.'

'Who's shouting now?'

Miles crossed his legs and flicked a moth off his trousers. She could have killed him, but before she had sat up enough to do anything undignified like throwing her shoes, Smith and the doctor arrived. Or rather the doctor arrived and Smith did his best to follow, but Miles gently shut the door in his face.

'I think the patient should be kept quiet, don't you, Doctor?' he said.

The doctor, an elderly Scotsman, agreed without paying any attention to Smith's disappointed expression. He was much rougher with her leg than Miles had been, less confident in his verdict. He wanted an X-ray next day.

When he left, Miles went with him.

'Look after yourself,' he said carelessly from the doorway. 'And I'll pop round when I can.'

'Please don't trouble – I shall be perfectly all right.'

Chapter Four

'Got yourself into another mess?' Michèle asked cheerfully, swinging her legs over the edge of the parapet.

Lucy was sitting out in the sun on her balcony with her ankle up on another chair.

'You talk as if I was always in a mess.'

'Well – aren't you?'

'Not that I know of – not more than you. I am noted for my efficiency.'

'Really?' Michèle looked politely astonished. 'In that case you'd better type out a monograph for old Smith on how the heat affected me. To my mind you've acted plain barmy the last few months.'

'Oh, nonsense – when?'

'Walking out on that jolly evening at Madame's, and the other jolly evening I arranged with Reginald and Charles, and not liking any of the Americans I introduce you to, and getting mixed up with Indians and wanting more work to do at the office, going off alone for the week-end, and now bicycling about in the dark by yourself and being run over.'

'I wasn't run over – I bumped into someone.'

'Same thing. If you'd been travelling home respectably with a gentleman friend in a tonga or a taxi it would never have happened.'

'The tonga might have become entangled with another tonga.'

'Oh, don't talk silly. Why can't you behave like the other girls out here? You are getting yourself talked about.'

'My morals are impeccable.'

'Morals,' said Michèle scornfully, laying a bottle of nail polish on the parapet. 'Who's interested in morals? Heaven knows I'm over in the American mess till all hours of the morning and nobody talks about me.'

'I shall make a point of talking about you in a shocked voice to everyone I meet.'

'No one will listen – it's what they expect of me. But you're making yourself the laughing-stock of the town.'

'Oh, Michèle, are you sure?'

'Dead sure. To be perfectly frank, you haven't got the looks to carry off your eccentricity.'

'But I'm not eccentric. I only wanted to find out what's going on,' she wailed.

'Take my advice and leave it alone. You're doing yourself no good with anyone. Sure you're not too ill to bear the smell of nail varnish?'

'No, do carry on,' she said faintly. 'And tell me why it should be a great big joke to want to meet people when you are living in their country.'

'I don't know. I'm not British, thank God, and the whole thing passes me by, but I'm quite quick at picking up what's done and what's not done in different countries, and I can clearly see that what you do is not done.'

'Hell!'

'Don't take it to heart and send your temperature up – just calm down and mend your ways.'

'What do you suggest I should do?'

'Go out with that nice major who was here all day on Thursday. What's wrong with him? He's British, over six foot, square in the shoulders, strong in the jaw, got plenty of hair and naughty eyes, and I shouldn't be surprised to hear he wears his own teeth.' Michèle finished painting one hand and held it out to dry.

'And when did you get close enough to note all this?'

'I had a good look when I came in to borrow a book off you when he was asleep.'

'How did you see his eyes?'

'I tripped against the chair and made rather a noise so he opened one eye, and if the other matches they're all right. I wouldn't mind taking him over myself if you're not interested. I don't go for the British as a rule, but he's better looking than most, and hasn't got one of those beastly moustaches. Where did you pick him up?'

'Oh, he's an old family friend. You can have him as far as I'm concerned. I've had my leg up for two days now and he hasn't even been round to enquire.'

Behaving on Monday as if he actually took a slight interest, she thought. Not that I care now. I don't like him anyway, but he did make one little link with home where they think I am ever so ordinary and nobody laughs at me.

'Michèle, do they really laugh out loud?'

'Who?'

'These people who are all talking about me. What do they say?'

'They say, "What's that dotty little golliwog girl done now?"'

'But it was *you* who told me to get my hair cut.'

'I didn't mean quite as short as *that*.'

'It'll grow – it's bound to. The sun makes everything grow.' She pulled desperately at one of her curls.

Michèle picked her handbag off the floor and began powdering her nose.

'Lash up the négligée,' she remarked, stretching her mouth for her lipstick. 'I see your major crossing the road.'

'Where?' she asked jumping to her feet, much too eagerly, and falling back with a squeak of pain without having seen anything.

'Out of sight now – coming upstairs.'

She hoped Michèle would be tactful and go away, but she only crossed her elegant brown legs and smiled provocatively at Miles as he came in. Lucy thought he looked a little surprised, and wondered if Michèle and Rachel could possibly be classed as the same type in the male mind. Apart from sex appeal she couldn't see they had anything in common.

Miles stopped staring at Michèle after a few seconds and stared at Lucy instead.

'You look better,' he said, without even apologising for not coming in before. She felt much worse straight away, and introduced him to Michèle.

'Going for a picnic?' Michèle asked, pointing to the hamper Miles had brought, but he opened it and handed Lucy a small black kitten.

'I thought it would last longer than flowers,' he said. The kitten walked round and round her knee and then settled down to sleep on her shoulder against her face.

Miles sat on the parapet and Lucy watched Michèle talking to him with very unusual animation. Lucy considered picking up a book to pass the time until Miles felt he knew Michèle well enough to take her out somewhere for dinner. But she restrained herself and lay back with her eyes on the concrete roof while the kitten purred into her ear.

Her bearer suddenly appeared with the hostel tin teapot, two cups and saucers, two small bits of bread and butter and two cakes. She could not be sure whose side he was on. He must have known perfectly well that she had two visitors, but he did not suggest fetching another cup. A few minutes later he slipped in again with a saucer of milk for the cat.

Miles did not move, so Michèle collected her bottle of varnish, her cotton-wool and her bag and clicked away in her fluffy pink mules, looking rather hurt.

'That's better,' Miles turned round to Lucy and picked up the teapot. 'Shall I pour? The cat's rather in your way. What a chatty girl.'

'She isn't usually – she was making a dead set at you. She thinks you are very good-looking and the only British gentleman in the town worth bothering about.'

'Dear me,' Miles tried not to look too pleased. 'I must be more indulgent to the poor girl should we ever meet again. What did the doctor decide about you?'

'Bad sprain, a few days' rest – just what you said.'

'Trust me another time?'

'Probably not.'

Later he opened his hamper again and lifted out a bottle of brandy and a couple of glasses.

'Purely medicinal, so you take it neat.'

'The cat must have been very uncomfortable in there.'

Brandy is an invigorating drink. After a couple of glasses she felt much better. Miles's profile looked altogether charming against the darkening sky. She tried hard to remember why she no longer liked him.

'Oh, Miles–' she sighed, too gently, and stopped. He turned his head.

'Hullo?'

'Do you like India?'

'Not much yet, but I expect to be going on to Burma soon and back to the real war, so I can stick it for a bit. What were you really going to say?'

'I was going to say... Do you think you'll ever get over Rachel?'

He looked angry again as soon as he heard her name.

'Of course I shall – don't be ridiculous – I'm young and healthy and I've no intention of letting her ruin my life. Has Priscilla written to you?'

'Not yet.'

'It doesn't matter anyway. There's nothing more to be said or heard about the whole sordid business. I'd be glad if you'd keep off it.'

She walked into that with her eyes open – why not accept the softening darkness, the softening drinks and Miles here and now without nagging? She held out her glass for some more brandy.

'Do you think Tiddim would be a good name for the kitten?'

'It's oriental and easily called. Is it still asleep?'

'Yes – where did you get it?'

'A man came to the mess with it. He wanted me to buy three.'

'Why didn't you?'

'Don't be greedy, one's plenty – I'm getting used to your hair now. I don't think it's *so* frightful after all. It's just rather extraordinary when I had always known you quiet and dark.' He looked at his watch. 'I must go.'

'Oh, don't – don't go – not just yet.'

'Must. Come again soon though.'

'Why not yesterday?'

'Working.'

She let go of his hand, surprised to find herself clinging to it.

'Excuse me,' she said stiffly. 'The dark is confusing. I thought it was my own.'

Miles laughed.

'Sweet thing – I'd forgotten how easy it was to intoxicate you.'

'Nonsense – I am not the least intoxicated. It was a natural mistake anyone could make in this light, or no light.'

'But my hand is much bigger.' Miles held it out solemnly. She studied it carefully and gave it back to him.

'You are perfectly right. My hands are small and elegant and did you know I have very good wrists?'

'I'm sure you have – now just stay there quietly till they bring you some supper.'

'My ankles are good too, Miles.'

'One of them is – the other is a bit off at the moment.'

She squinted down at her left leg.

'Oh yes – I'd forgotten all those bandages. Will you come back and see my ankles another time?'

'I'd be delighted, Miss Slade.'

'Please don't stand on ceremony. You may call me Lucy – all my friends do. I've got *lots* of friends, Miles.'

'I'm sure you have.'

'Lots and lots and lots of friends. What do you think one has – a gaggle of friends or a pride of friends?'

'I feel mine are a gaggle all right just now. Good night.' He kissed her on the forehead over the back of her chair.

'Pass, friend,' she waved her arm airily, and went on talking about the joys of companionship, the marriage of true minds and the pleasures of mixed nature rambles for some minutes before she noticed that she was talking to herself, so she finished the sentence with 'aren't they, Tiddim?' who had moved down to her knee, to put things right.

It would be fun to have a cat, cats don't laugh at people, only kings. Her eyes closed and she slept.

She woke sharply to a blood-curdling scream and in the darkness dimly saw an animal, looking as big as a tiger, loping away down the balcony with Tiddim hanging limply from its immense jaws. She jumped up and hopped after it screaming too, her bearer rushed in from the passage and headed off the tiger. She turned on the light and revealed a snarling tabby and the corpse of a black kitten with a bite right through its throat. So after all, even in India, flowers would have lasted longer.

Chapter Five

As winter drew on she bicycled to work in the dark and passed little groups of Indians who had slept by the road, lighting morning fires.

'There must be something to be done about them,' she said to Singh in the office. 'And all the people who sleep in the railway stations, where do they live?'

'In the railway stations, I expect,' Singh answered. 'And did you enjoy yourself dancing at the Imperial last night?'

'Not much. Were you there? Why didn't you come and say hullo?'

'I was with relations.'

'Singh, don't you care at all what happens to them?'

'To whom?'

'The hungry millions, the railway station people.'

'Did your countrymen care what happened to the Irish in 1847? – and what about Amritsar?'

'But these are your *own* countrymen – and anyway we are more enlightened now.'

'Are you? Your silly old war and the concentration camps and massacres in the ghettoes.'

'The British don't have concentration camps and massacres.'

Indians always said what about Amritsar. There seemed always to be no answer. She found as usual that she had been shuffled into a false position.

'Shut up, you two,' yelled McCleod, who was wearing ear-phones. 'Important bulletin coming through.'

Singh picked up the *New Yorker* again, and Lucy started another letter to Priscilla.

'The new bombs must be horrid,' she wrote. 'How do Rachel and Henry conduct their married life with one in the basement and the other upstairs, or has Rachel given him some of her courage?'

She sucked the end of her pen. London now seemed very far away.

'Miles is still here, but I don't see him much as I am too busy. I wish I could manage to go out with him more often as he is obviously depressed about Rachel and needs cheering up, but unfortunately–' unfortunately what? 'unfortunately I am a coward and afraid of being hurt.' She could see Miles every day, it surely wouldn't make her feel any worse than counting the minutes to each Wednesday night.

'Miles looks thinner,' she wrote – then scratched it out heavily – too much about Miles. Who cared except her if he looked as though he had not slept well for weeks.

Damn Rachel, damn all seductive women.

'They are opening a dispensary for the untouchables tonight,' Singh volunteered suddenly, without looking up from the *New Yorker*.

'Who is "they"?'

'Congress leaders. I shan't go, but why don't you if you are so keen on helping the poor Indians?'

'Where is it?'

'Somewhere just outside New Delhi, by the Purana Quila, I believe. You should get quite a bit of local colour.'

'What time?'

'Six-thirty.'

Wednesday night and Miles due to collect her at seven o'clock – but it shouldn't take long and with the speed of light on her repaired bicycle she could be back at the hostel soon after seven.

'I shall go,' she decided.

'You are an enterprising and inquisitive woman, Miss Slade,' Singh said in a voice of deep disapproval. 'If you really want to do any good to this country you would sail straight home.'

'Haven't enough money.'

He did not believe her.

'All the British have too much money.'

'Shut up – shut up – shut *up!*' McCleod thumped his fist on the table. 'If you can't find any work to do for God's sake get out and leave me to carry on alone in peace.'

She had planned to wear a new dress for Miles, but to be unobtrusive at the dispensary she covered her bare shoulders with a soft white Kashmir shawl; the evenings grew pleasantly chilly now after six o'clock. She told her bearer to ask Miles to wait in her room.

'At it again?' Michèle leant against the doorpost as she swung her bicycle out on to the gravel.

'At what?'

'Charging out in your best dress on a bicycle instead of waiting decently to be fetched by your escort.'

'I'm only going for a ride for half an hour.'

'Oh yes – *in* your new dress.'

'Why not? It has a nice wide skirt for pedalling.'

'It'll crease abominably. You are up to no good, Lucy.'

'Oh, don't nag. What does it matter to you?'

'Nothing – only I'd like to know where you are going so that I can dine out on it.'

'I'm off to the Purana Quila to shoot a rogue elephant.'

'*N'oubliez pas votre cheval*,' Michèle shouted after her, as with the usual difficulty she wrapped the folds of her dress round the bar of her man's bicycle and wobbled out of the gate, narrowly missing the toes of the doorkeeper who crouched on the ground in a trance with his beard dangling between his knees.

She found the place easily, but as she approached the huts the road was so blocked with people going in the same direction that she was forced to get off her bicycle and after a few minutes she chained the back wheel and abandoned it altogether.

The crowd seemed amiable but determined. She was too small to see over their heads and could only hope they were taking her towards the dispensary. The sun was setting behind the old red fort, and everywhere the smoke from evening fires rose straight up into a purple sky.

After being gently pushed forward for some minutes she found herself near the front, and indeed only a few yards from a small hut, very little larger than any of the huts, which appeared to be the goal. For at least half an hour nothing happened, the crowd swayed to and fro chatting and laughing. No one spoke to her. It was after seven – Miles would be already champing at the hostel – when the political leaders in their little white caps came slowly up through the crowd and the ceremony began.

There were several speeches, long speeches, before the last leader finally turned the key and flung the dispensary open. She could not understand one word and several times attempted to turn and find a way of escape, but she was firmly hemmed in and had to wait till the very end. When the people saw the door open they made a rush forward (perhaps to queue for the first surgery), and she felt a sudden chill round her shoulders. She put up her hand to find her shawl had vanished in the stampede. She could not see anyone near her wearing it – though so many people were dressed in white she might not have noticed it anyway. Now she was cold as well as frightened. She started to force her way back against the laughing, jostling Indians, but after struggling for ten minutes the road looked as far away as ever. It was nearly dark by now and faces melted into the night leaving only eyes and teeth and swirling white cotton all round. She fought against the certainty that she would faint and be softly trampled to death by thousands of sandals and gentle bare feet. Then thankfully she saw Miles, taller than anyone else, thrusting his way into the crowd. He could not see her. She stood on tiptoe and waved and shouted frantically till at last, above the other excited voices, he heard.

He seized her hand roughly and began to pull her back behind him, making a path so easily that she was jerked along and almost running.

'Oh, please, not so fast,' she panted, bumping up against him, but he didn't say a word and only walked faster. She heard the people near beginning to murmur crossly, as they had not done when she was alone.

'Miles, can't you see how rude you are being to them? Don't knock them about as if they were sheep.'

But he didn't answer that one either, and in five minutes they stood side by side on the road again. Miles had a tonga waiting and practically threw her into it.

'My bicycle!' she shrieked as she was carried away at a smart trot.

'Damn your bicycle.'

'But I must have it. I can't get to work in the morning without it.'

'Where is it?'

'Somewhere near here – honestly – do stop.'

She jumped down and ran along the edge of the road trying to remember. By a ruined shrine, was it? Or by a tree? Or by a tethered goat?

Miles strode up and down the other side and she could see rage gathering with every movement. There was, of course, no bicycle. It had been stolen ages ago.

'All right, never mind. I'm sorry, Miles. It doesn't matter.'

She pulled his arm, but he wouldn't come.

'Of course it matters, a bicycle is an expensive item. Just remember exactly where you put it.'

'I can't – everywhere looks the same. It's so dark now.'

'My dear Lucy, you must at least remember which side of the road you dropped it?'

'I don't. There were so many people, I couldn't really see either side.'

They stood in the middle of the road and she waited for the storm to break. The tonga driver huddled over his horse, idly flicking its ears with his whip. A small, pale moon drifted free of the branches behind Miles's head.

'What did you think you were doing out here in the first place?'

'They opened a dispensary.'

'What's that got to do with you?'

'It's interesting – they don't open many dispensaries.'

'Do you realise you might have been killed?'

'Why should I be? They were perfectly kind and quiet until you came and started throwing your weight about.'

'European women don't do that sort of thing.'

'Why not?'

Miles lost his temper completely.

'They just don't, and above all they don't parade about alone in a crowd, half-naked.'

'How dare you talk to me like that?'

Her voice rose too. She couldn't tell him about the shawl now as she had been so busy defending the kindness of the people.

'I'll talk to you how I like, you stupid little half-wit.' He suddenly leaned forward and, grasping her shoulders, gave her a good shake. She tried to slap his face but only succeeded in thumping his chest. It flashed through her mind that with all these nursery tactics she might as well bite him, but before she could get at him he let her go and she said in a shaking voice:

'Look – we're behaving like a couple of children.'

'Who started it?' Miles asked sulkily. He looked very funny with his hair ruffled. 'I've never heard of anything more childish and irresponsible than the way you went off this evening, leaving me to pick you out of the mess.'

'I never asked you to. I left a message for you to wait.'

'Luckily for you, your bearer had more sense. He told me you shouldn't have gone and advised me to chase after you.'

'Thank you very much, I'm sure, for saving my life,' she said, thoroughly irritated. 'As the flashing curved knives closed around me I knew my last hour had come, but whom did I see galloping to my rescue, careless of his own safety, but my shining hero.'

Miles slapped her face. It was a much more efficient slap than hers. She could not blame him, but it hurt and she burst into tears.

'Oh, no–' Miles sounded completely exasperated to have a crying female on his hands on top of everything else. He was not a man to be softened by tears as she very well knew, but she could not stop.

'Boohoo, I wish I was dead,' she moaned feebly, swaying in the middle of the road, but not wanting to annoy Miles any further by crying on his shoulder and making his chest damp.

'Shall we go and have a drink?' Miles suggested, cold and reasonable. He climbed into the tonga and she followed snivelling.

'I suppose you haven't got a hankie?' Miles's voice was colder still. She shook her head, unable to answer, and he passed her a clean one. She had taken out nothing but her shawl.

'Please stop at the hostel,' she said when she could manage to speak without gulping. 'I shall want a coat or something.'

The most dignified thing to do would be to end the evening here and now. Step down, turn round, shake hands politely and finish the whole thing; but she wanted to see him at any price, better furious than not at all, and after tonight he would clearly never ask her out again.

She kept him waiting only five minutes. She wouldn't have been as long as that, but she met Michèle on the stairs again coming down with her American. She tried to slither past them, but they stopped her under the light half-way up.

'Caught cold now?' Michèle asked. 'Told you you shouldn't go bicycling in the dark?'

'Terrible hurry,' she muttered. 'See you later.'

'Did you catch that elephant?' Michèle called after her.

'Shot him dead between the tusks,' she answered.

Her face looked worse even than she imagined. Fear and tears had turned it blotchy. She did what she could with powder and returned to Miles in calm despair.

He was looking at his watch and as cross as ever, and they drove the rest of the way to the hotel in complete silence. She held her head up very straight and recited Gray's Elegy to herself.

Just before they arrived Miles looked at her curiously.

'What's the matter, Lucy?'

'Nothing – why?'

'You're muttering.'

'Was I?'

'Do you feel all right?'

'Yes, thank you.'

But he was kinder to her after that and

ordered her a large brandy.

'I'm sorry I was a nuisance,' she admitted a little while later.

'It's not so much being a nuisance, but you must realise that it's serious, and possibly dangerous, to get mixed up in politics. That sort of behaviour makes both sides suspicious.'

'I only wanted to see what was happening. It's nothing to do with politics.'

'That may be the truth for you, but the Indians as well as the British will think you are up to no good and going to cause trouble. Everything here now is politics.'

'How do you know?'

'People tell me things.'

'How many Indian friends have you?'

'That's beside the point.'

'Don't you see it's the whole point? You only hear the official British view – you've got nothing to balance it against.

'You talk as if the whole thing were reasonable – views on each side, to be appreciated. Don't you understand that reason has long ago disappeared and everything now is reduced to emotions?'

'But just because everyone else is emotional why should you, a sensible, intelligent doctor, abandon reason too?'

'I don't know – I only know that there aren't enough European women out here, that their actions are far more important than they were at home and that when I hear you are making a fool of yourself it drives me berserk.'

'I've always wondered how that was pronounced.'

Miles looked furious again, but she tried hard not to laugh at him.

'Come on,' he stood up. 'Let's forget the whole thing, and dance.'

'You are as bad as Singh,' she said, slipping far too comfortably into his arms.

Miles stiffened.

'Who is Singh?'

'A Sikh I know.'

He swept her savagely round the room.

'You don't go out with him, I hope?' he asked after the first circuit.

'With whom?'

'This Sikh.'

'He hasn't asked me yet.'

Miles's grip on her tightened. She knew it was only annoyance, but she took advantage of it all the same and leant heavily against him. He danced very well, she closed her eyes and moved in a delicious dream until he caught her out on a difficult corner. She fell over his left leg and nearly overbalanced.

'Wake up,' Miles snapped. 'Keep your mind on your footwork. You can't pretend the day at your office tires you out.'

'I was just relaxing.'

'Don't – you aren't a good enough dancer

to relax.'

'Why do you have to be so rude to me all the time?'

'I'm not rude.'

'You are so.'

'Oh, really–' Miles stopped dead. 'Are we or are we not dancing a waltz?'

'Apparently you are and I'm not – unless this is a particularly interesting hesitation step that I'm not following.'

'I've a good mind to shake you again.'

'Oh no, you can't do that.'

'Why not?'

They still stood in the centre of the room with other couples bouncing round them. Miles had not taken his arm away from her, but the look on his face was far from friendly.

'Because,' she said, hanging herself for a sheep, 'European men don't do that sort of thing out here to their precious European women.'

She thought he would have some sort of seizure. He turned almost purple under his normal tan and walked back to their table without speaking, she hustled after trying to look as if she was with him. He ordered two more brandies and sat staring at a spot on the floor about three feet away. She wished she had brought something to read.

'Close for the time of year,' she ventured after five minutes. But it didn't go down well, never any good at letting sulking dogs lie, she followed up with:

'Heard from Priscilla this week?' an even more unsuccessful joke. Miles made a sort of growling noise which sounded so inhuman he quickly changed it to a cough and added as an afterthought:

'No.'

After this there was another ten minutes' silence. She sipped her brandy slowly. It was by now well after nine o'clock and it didn't look as if they were going to have any supper. From the dining-room across the hall came the scent of chickens turning on their spits. Her mouth watered. She noted all these sensations with interest and realised that Miles's moronic behaviour this evening had finally disillusioned her. One couldn't surely be in love with a person if in the middle of a first-class row one's mind was transfixed by roasting chickens.

She turned on Miles a smile of such sudden radiance at this internal discovery that he looked quite startled.

'Let's eat,' she urged.

He made a great effort and smiled back.

Chapter Six

McCleod asked her to go to a Hogmanay dance.

'I didn't know you liked dancing?'

'I don't, but they will have reels and sensible stuff.'

'Very interesting local colour for Miss Slade,' said Singh. 'Why don't you try to colonise the wild Scotsmen?'

'Will you wear a kilt?' she asked McCleod.

'Of course.'

Not only a kilt, but also a dagger. He danced like a demon with loud whoops and yells, brandishing his beard. He confused her sadly and she found herself going the wrong way round the chains and dashing when other white sergeants were retreating. The respites at the bar were not reassuring either, as McCleod drank whisky as if it were lemonade. She nodded frostily to Miles who seemed to be alone.

After this third whisky McCleod asked her to marry him. He asked her at the top of his strong voice in the middle of the bar.

'Come on, let's dance,' she tried to laugh it off, 'look, the eightsome has begun.'

'Lucy, you don't take me seriously – I

mean it.'

'Ask me again in the morning.'

'The morning is no time for romance. The hot fighting blood of the McCleods is up *now.*'

'Marriage isn't fighting. I want to dance.' She dragged him back towards the dance floor.

'If you marry me it will be dancing and fighting all the time – say "Yes".' He would not move another step.

She could see Miles on his stool at the bar laughing heartily.

McCleod was getting more dangerous every minute. He suddenly drew his dagger and started walking up and down in front of her shouting: 'I want this woman and who shall say me nay?'

Nobody said him nay. At the sight of the naked knife everybody backed to the other end of the room. And all the time Miles was watching her humiliation.

'Now,' said McCleod, 'you are at my mercy. My wife or my knife – which is it to be?'

'Do you want me to call the police? Do be quiet – you're drunk.'

'Aha – you can't call the police, you can't call anyone unless I say so. Come on, lovely Lucy.'

Out of the corner of her eye she saw Miles leave the bar with a resigned expression. He

93

strolled up to them, and stood over McCleod.

'Better pack it in, old man – don't want a fuss here.'

But McCleod was not to be bullied by superior size and strength. He had the advantage of being armed. He lunged unexpectedly at Miles. Miles, instead of moving sideways to avoid the knife, seized the blade with his bare hand and twisted it away.

A woman behind them screamed, there was a rush for the doors, someone started shouting for a doctor. McCleod sobered up instantly, and Miles stood there looking rather surprised while the blood dripped steadily from his hand on to the carpet.

'Why do you keep it so sharp?' he asked McCleod.

'You fool,' snapped McCleod, 'of course it's sharp – here, give it back to me. I'll put it away before it causes any more trouble.' He spoke as if Miles was the one who had been waving it about.

Lucy felt in Miles's pockets and found a clean handkerchief – she tried to act professionally, but her hands were shaking so much she couldn't knot the bandage.

'You wouldn't make a good nurse if the sight of blood upsets you,' Miles remarked. 'Here, I'll do it myself.'

'Shall I tear up my dress? That isn't going

to be enough.'

'No, for goodnes sake, don't make any further exhibition of yourself. They are sure to find a doctor in a minute or two, and if they don't I'll go round to the hospital.'

'Oh, Miles, don't be unfair. How could I know he would get so drunk?'

'You might have guessed. It looks as though I shall have to see you home.'

McCleod had silently disappeared with his dagger.

'Don't be ridiculous. I shall see you to the hospital. I'm sure you are going to need stitches in that cut.'

He looked faint, so she took his arm firmly and led him towards the door, and even more firmly into a taxi. The military hospital was several miles outside the town. She held his uninjured hand during the ride and made bracing conversation to which he replied in monosyllables, but the cut hurt badly because every now and again he gripped her hand as if he would break the bones.

When they arrived he said good night to her at the front door and added, patting her on the shoulder:

'You're all right, really, Lucy.'

She turned away, though she had no intention of leaving, and sat down on the edge of the veranda to wait. The taxi-driver settled on the step of his taxi and they both stared at the moon. Inside the hospital she could hear someone moaning. She hoped they would give Miles an anæsthetic.

They must have waited nearly an hour before he returned, the taxi-driver had fallen asleep, and she had torn a strip off the hem of her dress. Miles wore a sling as well as a bandage.

'I never thought you'd wait, Lucy.'

'Wanted to be sure you were intact.'

'They nearly put me to bed in there.'

'I was going in to inquire, if you hadn't come soon. I shouldn't have waited all night, but it's early yet, only 1 a.m.'

'What a pity, you missed Auld lang syne.'

'Not much loss. I'd lost my partner anyway.'

'What are we standing about for? Let's go home.'

He woke the driver and told him to drive to her hostel.

'Nonsense,' she said, 'we drop you off first tonight.'

After some mild objections he agreed. He put his good arm round her in the car.

'You know, it might be quite a good idea if you married me, Lucy,' he remarked, in the voice of one suggesting an outing to the zoo.

'Why?'

'We're old friends, aren't we? And like each other very much, and if you were my wife I could keep you out of trouble better.'

As a proposal it was even drearier than McCleod's, who had at least offered dancing.

'I don't think it would work, Miles.'

'Why not?'

'It doesn't sound very gay?'

She made her voice light, but she was cold and sick inside and the drive seemed interminable.

'Wednesday, as usual?' Miles asked when the taxi stopped.

She managed: 'Of course – seven o'clock?' in a matter-of-fact voice before he had quickly kissed her good night, slammed the door, and waved the driver on again.

It is an odd agony to be offered your heart's desire on a plate like a chilled fried egg. For two years she had wanted to marry Miles, but not as a business proposition.

McCleod was very apologetic in the office and gave her extra work to do, but they neither of them alluded to his proposal again. She made enquiries about joining a canteen force in Burma since there seemed to be no sign of a posting for Miles, and she felt one of them would have to leave Delhi.

She went for two picnics, one delicious, with Indian friends, to the gardens of an old mosque where they sat by water in the shade of wide trees; and one horrible with Michèle and two Americans to the banks of the

Jumna River where they sat on muddy sand by prickly bushes, and saw an old man go by, once with a hatchet, and the second time with a hatchet in one hand and a fat black snake in the other. The Americans had brought whisky, but they bought lemonade for Lucy at a little stall inland. The bottle was unaccountably marked 'Made in Japan'.

She was soon lost in the wisecracks and felt stupid and priggish and too hot in the sun. For a time they tried to draw her in, but they gave it up in the end and left her in peace. Michèle and her friend wandered off down the banks of the river, and abandoned Lucy to the other one who, after a short routine attempt at seduction, became frankly bored, and lay back with a handkerchief over his sallow face and fell asleep. She had learnt, however, that situations like this developed all too often in India so she always carried a book now, and passed the next hour relatively agreeably in *Northanger Abbey* behind her sun-glasses.

When in the middle of February Miles also suggested a picnic she at first refused.

'Why not?'

'Indian picnics are horrid.'

'Not always.'

'The last one I went on was, too much sun, too much sand, and a large dead snake.'

'I promise you I'll do better than that. Not a single snake, alive or dead. I'll come at noon on Sunday.'

Miles's hand was still stiff so he brought his bearer to carry the picnic basket.

'Lucky you aren't a surgeon,' she said looking at the hand.

'Pity really – I'd have been insured for vast sums. It'll be all right in another month.'

They drove to the gardens of a mosque. The bearer laid a rug for them on the grass at the foot of a flight of marble steps and ran round filling wine-glasses and breaking up chips of ice and handing chicken. There was no sand, no wasp, no snake to mar the pleasure. Afterwards Miles dispatched the bearer with the debris.

'Do you think it's snowing at home?' she asked with a bed of scarlet flowers flaring in front of her. Miles lay flat on his back with his hands behind his head.

'If not snowing it's surely raining in February. This is the sort of sun and, round the corner of the mosque, the sort of wind you ought to get and never do at the English seaside in August. Come on.'

He jumped up.

'I shall fall asleep if we don't do something. Shall we explore the mosque?'

She'd have been happy to sleep, but she obediently got to her feet and followed him up the dark twisting staircase to the platform where they used to call the faithful to prayer.

They could see most of New Delhi stiffly stretched out below from its central circle. Miles narrowed his eyes and looked out across the plain.

'I should be going soon,' he said.

'Burma?'

'I suppose so – or Japan.'

'Oh, Miles.'

'I'll be thankful – this town is eating me up.'

He did not look at her and she tried to drag her stricken face back to polite interest.

'Will you write to me?' she asked, trying not to sound eager.

'I'm not much good at writing letters.'

'Couldn't you try?'

'Don't see the point, if I don't enjoy it.'

'Shall I write to you?'

'Do, if you feel like it, and don't mind going without an answer.'

'I might just let you know how things are going, occasionally. I don't suppose I'll have much time really.'

Miles seemed to swallow this enormous lie quite easily, though he must have known she'd have written to him every night with the smallest encouragement.

He led the way down the spiral staircase and at the darkest corner turned to hold out a hand to her at the same moment as she missed a step and fell forward into his arms.

After several minutes Miles took his

mouth away from hers.

She whispered 'I love you so' to the pockets on his tunic. Miles didn't answer, he only tilted her head back and began to kiss her again.

'I've wanted to do that for such a long time,' he said at last. 'Now will you marry me?'

'Yes – please – soon.'

He tried to hold her away to let the light filtering up the staircase from below illuminate her face, but she didn't want him to look at her yet, and clasped her hands round his neck. He laughed and they kissed again.

Dimly, she could hear footsteps on the stairs, but she was still lost in Miles when someone tapped her on the shoulder and a gentle Indian voice said: 'Excuse, please, may we come in?' They both raised their heads to see an embarrassed couple, he in a white shirt with tail out over blue trousers, and she in an emerald-green *sari*, hesitating on the step below them.

'Why,' Lucy said, astonished, 'no one can get past us.'

'Nor they can,' agreed Miles. He drew her over to stand beside him and the Indians trotted quickly up without a backward glance.

Miles laughed.

'Did you see his face?'

'Poor little man, they think we are terribly wicked.'

'Nothing wicked about you and me. Wasn't that the first time I've kissed you?'

'Yes, Miles.'

'Can't think why I didn't try it before.'

'Neither can I, Miles.'

'Besides, we're engaged, aren't we?'

'Are we?'

'Well – we can't get married without being engaged. Unless we get married tonight. Shall we do that?'

He took her hand and rushed her down the stairs out into the sunlight without waiting for an answer.

'That's better,' he said straightening his shoulders. 'I was getting fibrositis leaning against that stone wall. What did you say?'

'I didn't say anything – yet–'

'Hurry up then – why not tonight?'

'Oh, darling, thousands of reasons – my aunts, your mother, our friends, I've applied to go to Burma, you are just going to be posted, we shall never meet again anyway.'

'Down with aunts, families, friends – we don't need them for a good wedding. Champagne is enough and I suppose we can find some somewhere in this terrible town. You must cancel your Burmese application, and I'm due for three weeks' leave before my posting anyway.'

'I can't,' she wailed. 'It's gone through.

They are expecting me at the end of April –
I'd be shot for deserting and I'm in the
middle of a long row with the Ministry
about leaving them.'

Miles sat down at the top of the marble
steps.

'Oh, Lucy,' he said, and the exhilaration
had gone out of his voice. 'Why did you
want to land yourself in another muddle?
Couldn't you have asked me about it first?'

'I didn't want to tell you till it was all
arranged.'

'But why Burma?'

'I wanted to get away from you.'

'But I shall probably be *in* Burma.'

'It didn't look like it when I started fixing
things up last month.'

She stood in front of him twisting her
handkerchief. Suddenly he looked up and
smiled:

'Understand this, goose, from now on I'm
in charge.'

'Lovely, lovely – but please may I go on
going to Burma and then we can be there
together?'

'What do you think you are going to do in
the jungle?'

'Dispense tea and hope and sausage rolls.'

Miles admitted grudgingly that there
might be no harm in it, provided there was
no likelihood of girls coming anywhere near
the front line. She had inquired closely into

this, and could assure him the canteens were established well to the rear. She sat down by Miles.

'O.K. then, Burma is on,' he said, very practical, 'and between now and then we get married and have a sensational honeymoon – Bombay with night life and warm sea bathing, or the eternal snows?'

'Mountains, please. Could we go to Tibet?'

But she had annoyed him again.

'Don't be so romantic. You have to spend three weeks in the saddle before you even *arrive* in Tibet and we shall only have three weeks to spare all told.'

'Somewhere near Tibet then, please.'

'All right, leave it to me.'

She found herself agreeing to a wedding at the end of the month. 'In that pleasant church in Old Delhi, please.'

Miles wanted a registry office, but she felt that without any familiar faces round her the whole thing would seem too unreal. Miles swallowed the church in the end.

'Then straight on to the night train for the hills,' he urged. She tried feebly for a day's respite in a Delhi hotel, but Miles felt about Delhi as she did about registry offices. 'We want to get right away,' he said firmly.

After half an hour their immediate future was settled.

'Now you are not to worry and not to *do* anything. I shall fix everything.'

104

'Yes, Miles.'

'I'll get the banns up, buy the tickets, take hotel rooms, square McCleod for your leave, argue with the Ministry, settle with the Burmese forces. Promise me you won't move hand or foot?'

'No, Miles. Except I must have some new clothes and a proper wedding-dress.'

'What, white, you mean?'

'Yes, please—'

'It hardly seems worth it with no guests.'

'Please — I shan't feel married without. I shall want Michèle to come anyway, and McCleod.'

Miles gave in over the dress. They went back to the hostel and planned until nightfall. Miles left very late for dinner in his mess after extracting one last promise.

'Darling, this is serious, before I go I want to be sure that now you are going to marry me you'll keep out of trouble and not do anything conspicuous.'

As she would be with Miles until she went to Burma it seemed safe to forswear trouble.

'Has Miles proposed yet?' Michèle asked, later in the evening.

'How did you guess?'

'He's obviously been on the verge of it for weeks if you hadn't scared him off, acting so peculiar, and I've never seen anyone gawp so much as you do when you look at him.'

'Surely,' she said coldly, 'my feelings

weren't as clear as all that?'

'Clearer,' Michèle answered. 'Anyway – I'm off with Sam to Calcutta at the end of next month, so I hope you've made your mind up now.'

'Oh, good – let's have a double wedding.'

'Wedding – my foot – Sam's got a nice wife and a couple of kids back in Kentucky.'

'Oh, poor Michèle.'

'I don't care – who knows what'll happen in six months anyway? But I'll come and have a good cry at your wedding and think of the pleasures of normal domesticity.'

'It won't be very normal in the Himalayas and we are both going to Burma afterwards.'

When Michèle had gone, she wrote to Priscilla.

'DEAR PRISCILLA,

'How are you all? Is Alan back yet? A lot has been happening here since Christmas, and now I am going to marry Miles. He suddenly asked me today. Please will you tell Rachel in case she might be interested. I wish you could be here for the wedding, it will all be very odd. Do you think my aunts will like Miles? I don't see how they can help it really. Doctors are so reliable and he's sure to have a steady income after the war– '

She sucked the end of her pen – the idea of Miles with a steady income seemed very funny.

'I am going to have a dress made of clouds of white organdie, hopelessly unuseful afterwards, but at least one can be sure it won't be raining here and it will look good for one afternoon.'

She fell asleep in billowing folds of white.

Chapter Seven

The *derzi* called nearly every day to fit her dress and unroll yards of lawn and silk for the trousseau at her feet.

Miles smoothed their path in all directions. McCleod offered to give her away. She accepted on condition he didn't drink a drop till after the ceremony. Michèle agreed to act as an unofficial bridesmaid, but refused a new dress.

'I've got six evening dresses,' she pointed out, 'surely one will be grand enough for you?'

Lucy inspected her wardrobe and they decided on a full-skirted yellow silk. Lucy would carry white roses and Michèle red.

'Very tasty, *ma chère* – may Sam come, or would his presence offend the odour of sanctity?'

Lucy said they'd be delighted to welcome Sam. The party was growing all the time. Miles moved the reception from his mess to the Cecil Hotel.

She slept badly on the last night in the hostel. She woke about six o'clock, got up and walked about restlessly in her nightdress. Her new dressing-gown was packed.

Her luggage stood in two piles on opposite sides of the room. A small suitcase and a holdall for the honeymoon, and a tin trunk and two large suitcases waiting to go into store in Delhi. She stood considering the luggage, so many new belongings in a few short months, she was hopelessly encumbered for another fresh start. She tore at the cord knotting up the trunk with sudden decision and ten minutes later her bearer, arriving with a cup of tea, looked horrified to see clothes all over the bed and all over the floor.

'*Mem-sahib* busy?' he asked, waiting for instructions. He had corded up the trunk very efficiently last night.

'I want to give all these things away,' she announced, feverishly, jumbling shoes, books, ribbons, blouses and cosmetics around her feet. Why had she not done this months ago? Finding Miles in her room had made her forget her good intentions, but it was not too late. The poor of Delhi should yet benefit from her generosity.

'Find poor people,' she commanded

'Please?'

'Tell people, Indian people who need these things, to come here.'

'I take away?'

'No, no, not all for you, bring many people to share and stand below in the courtyard.'

The bearer saluted and withdrew.

She dragged and kicked her discarded worldly goods on to the balcony and laid them out in rows along the parapet. She had not long to wait. The bearer may have rounded up his relations or only the hotel servants, but within ten minutes a murmuring, excited crowd had gathered below. It was not yet seven o'clock.

'Who wants these?' she called, holding up a pair of sandals. Six hands stretched out and she threw them into the middle. 'And these?' two old jerseys followed. 'And this?' A half-empty bottle of talcum powder.

The struggling and screaming grew, stronger. She hurled things down as fast as she could. There was a nasty moment when she hit an elderly gentleman with an old galosh, but he rallied splendidly, though not in time to catch the second galosh.

She felt fine, as good as St. Francis. She pushed her hair out of her eyes and took a long swing back for a pair of heavy china book-ends, but her arms were seized from behind, the crowd grew suddenly quiet, and she twisted round to find herself looking at Miles. He marched her back into the room, and slammed both doors. She realised with a sinking heart that he was more angry than ever.

'Have you gone out of your mind?'

'I was only giving away some old things.'

'But why to a football crowd, with fifty

people watching from every hostel window and more in the road? Do you realise – I guessed something was up by the people outside pushing to get in, and one man came out wearing a *petticoat* on his *head*.'

'Did he look very funny?'

'Oh, Lucy – for God's sake – you promised me you wouldn't do anything else till we were married.'

'Surely it's not so very awful to clear out some of my junk?'

'Why couldn't you put it in the waste-paper basket, or give it to your bearer?'

'It didn't seem fair he should have everything.'

'What about me?'

'What about you? You surely didn't want my bookends?'

'No – no. I mean making a fool of me.'

'You weren't even *there,*' she said, puzzled.

Miles tried to speak gently.

'Lucy, at three o'clock this afternoon you and I are getting married–' he began, but she interrupted him with sudden horror.

'Oh, darling, you shouldn't *be* here – we shouldn't meet beforehand, it's terribly unlucky, you must go now. Perhaps it doesn't count before eight? What were you doing out in the road so early anyway?'

'Couldn't sleep,' Miles mumbled, looked dejected. 'Look, darling, are you sure you really *want* to get married?'

'Miles – what do you mean?'

'I just wondered whether you were ever going to feel like doing the sort of things I like doing.'

'But of course I shall. I shall be a terribly energetic doctor's wife, answering the telephone, and making you meals in the middle of the night.'

'Yes, but do you think you'll remember that there are two of us and that when you take a foolish action, you take it as for me?'

'Of course – oh, darling, I will try, I'm sure it'll be all right. But please go now and shut your eyes passing round the cupboard, you mustn't see my dress hanging on the end.'

Miles sighed, kissed her abruptly and she was left alone with an empty trunk, two china book-ends and an old pair of bedroom slippers. The recipients of her charity had melted away.

Lucy, McCleod and Michèle left the hostel together in a taxi at twenty minutes to three, cheered from every window.

'Tell the driver to go slowly,' Lucy asked McCleod. 'We mustn't be early.' She inclined graciously to her well-wishers. She had to lean forward anyway to keep the weight off her organdie.

'Have you got indigestion?' McCleod asked.

'She didn't eat any lunch so she can't

have,' Michèle told him.

'No lunch?' McCleod looked worried. 'Can't get married on an empty stomach – have a swig of this.' He brought a flask out of his pocket.

'Oh, you promised not to drink till afterwards.'

'I shan't – it's quite unbroached, I brought it specially for you – emergency ration– Go on.'

'I will if you won't, Lucy,' Michèle stretched out her hand.

'I think the bride should have first lick,' McCleod said.

Lucy took it from him and obediently put it to her lips. She flung her head back too far and, in her anxiety to keep the drips away from her fichu, swallowed more than she intended.

The taxi proceeded regally at twenty miles an hour down the long straight road to Old Delhi, past huts and tents and the civilian hospital, till at last the red fort came in sight.

'I think we could go faster now, don't you?' she suggested. The brandy had burned away her nerves. McCleod spoke to the driver who nodded his head and pressed his foot on the accelerator. The car at once stopped dead.

'He didn't understand you. He must have thought you told him to brake.'

'Go on faster!' McCleod shouted in Hindustani, but the driver ignored them all. He climbed down laboriously, his turban wobbling, and disappeared into the bonnet. They heard a faint, far-away knocking. The driver's friend, who sat beside him, turned and assured them that the driver was very attached to his motor.

'Oh, do something, do something,' Lucy moaned.

McCleod shouted that they didn't care how fond he was of his motor, they wanted to see it *go*.

'Motor goes very fast,' the friend replied, hurt.

'You help him,' McCleod ordered. So the friend, still looking injured and without removing his cigarette, climbed out on the other side and lay down in the road under the car. He had taken no knocking implement with him and it was clear that he planned to fire the petrol tank.

They talked matily to each other through the intestines of the car. Presumably the driver could not actually see his friend. Presently the driver walked round and made two desultory turns on the starting-handle. The friend gave a sharp yelp, but there was no sound from the engine.

Lucy's hands were sweating, she bounded up and down, forgetful of her organdie.

'Let's walk – it's not more than five

minutes from here.'

'I'll just see if I can fix the car myself.'

McCleod got over into the driving-seat and pulled out all the knobs. The driver seemed to have forgotten them and was busy helping his friend out and dusting him down. The friend had pinched his finger, and was very upset and chatty.

Lucy could not bear the inactivity any longer. She struggled over Michèle's long skirt and out, and peered into the works.

'Can you flush the carburettor?' McCleod called.

She fiddled with one or two plugs before admitting that the carburettor was a stranger to her.

'Abandon ship then,' said McCleod, slamming the door behind him, 'and no rupees either.'

'I *can't* walk,' Michèle complained, 'my shoes are much too flimsy.'

'We'll walk till we see another taxi or a tonga. Bound to be one along in a minute.'

'What's the time?' Lucy asked.

'Five past three.'

'Oh, no. Oh, Miles will be furious.' She gathered up her skirts and began to run.

'The flowers—' Michèle screamed. 'We've forgotten the flowers.'

With a poorly stifled oath, McCleod trotted back to the car for the bouquets. When he caught them up again he reported that he had left the driver and friend sitting side by side on the running-board reading a newspaper. Lucy had settled into a steady, loping gallop, they could now see the church in the distance.

'I can't possibly keep up,' yelled Michèle. 'I'll meet you at the reception.'

McCleod was making slightly better time than Lucy, a kilt being a far more practical garment for running than an ankle-length, full-skirted wedding-dress and veil. He finally beat her to the church door by about five yards. She drew in level with a tonga which had been trying to attract her attention for several minutes. Michèle made a very poor third.

Miles stood in the porch, very starched in his best uniform, with his hair almost flat, studying his watch. For a wild moment Lucy imagined he might be genially timing their performance. Then he looked up and took in the appearance of the bridal party and the mild reproof he had been about to deliver for ordinary lateness stuck in his throat. She looked at the others. McCleod's beard had blown into a dishevelled tangle. He was mopping the sweat from his face with a filthy grey handkerchief. He had stuffed the two bouquets through the strings of his sporran in order to have his hands free. Michèle, though not quite so red, was panting loudly and had taken off a

116

shoe to examine the damage.

Finally Miles managed to stutter, and she had never heard him stutter before. 'Lucy, your *face*,' then he added in a fainter voice, 'and your dress – why on earth did you choose white?'

She put her hand doubtfully to her face. It seemed unfair to pick on her when the others looked so freakish.

'Don't–' implored Michèle. 'You're making it worse.'

She held up the glass from her handbag and Lucy saw, with horror, that she wore a long streak of black oil from forehead to chin, and, following Miles's downward glance, two more streaks across the front of the organdie where she had leant against the car. Behind them all the organ repeated placidly the tune of 'Sheep may safely graze', also Lucy's choice.

'I'll clean you up,' Michèle said briskly. Miles turned his back on them without another word and marched away up the aisle. Michèle got to work with her handkerchief, which through the blur of sweat and tears Lucy was glad to notice was several shades cleaner than McCleod's. 'You are not to cry. Stop it at once or I shall be wasting my time.'

'Miles is so angry,' she sniffed, 'I don't think I can bear to go up there to the altar.'

'Nonsense. He's only upset because he's

nervous too, and nobody likes to be kept waiting. Thank goodness you didn't lose your veil in the rush anyway. Now stand still while I put the wreath straight. Did you know it had slipped over one ear?'

Michèle lowered the veil to hide her red eyes, and cleverly pinned a fold of material across so that the marks on her dress didn't show either.

'*Ca va, chèrie*. You look marvellous. *Allons-y.*'

'And likewise Scots wha hae,' said McCleod gallantly, offering his arm. In the doorway they stopped again while he disentangled the bruised roses from his sporran. At last they entered, with proper dignity and downcast eyes, not more than twenty minutes late.

The champagne was a good vintage, in spite of the war, in spite of India, laid down many years ago. Miles began to smile after his second glass. Lucy's colleagues from the office were as friendly as could be, although on paper she was now engaged in a private war with them about her release, her passage money and her clothing allowance. Her married face seemed an improvement on the one she had left at the church door.

'Time to change,' Miles said, looking at his watch, but not sternly.

Michèle took her up to the hotel bedroom

118

where the travelling clothes lay waiting.

'Is it honestly the first time?' she asked, unbuttoning the white dress at the back.

'Yes–' Lucy mumbled, through a mouthful of veil.

'Well, don't worry, dear, there's nothing like it in the whole wide world.'

'No – I suppose not. I wasn't worrying – much.'

'That's the girl.'

'Nothing like it for better, not for worse?'

'For more than better, for *champs élysées*.'

'With anyone?'

'Loving helps.'

'I ought to love Miles enough for anything – but I did wonder whether I might not just be rather bad at it?'

'You're sure to learn fast and Miles looks a good teacher.'

'Thank you, Michèle. You're a fine brides-maid, acting as the bride's mother as well.'

Michèle, McCleod, Irene, and Miles's best man saw them to the train and put three more bottles of champagne on top of their luggage. McCleod did a sword-dance on the platform, but as he wasn't wearing his dagger nobody tried to stop him. Everyone was laughing and shouting and when the train drew slowly out of the station the sudden silence of being alone in the carriage with Miles startled her.

'Well,' Miles said heartily, bringing his head in and looking round for something to organise.

'Well,' she replied, only more feebly, sitting down in the arm-chair provided by the railway company.

Miles moved a suitcase or two which had been perfectly well arranged by his bearer, and took her bouquet across to the washbasin. She went on sitting, it seemed another moment at which a good thriller would have come in handy. She remembered with regret that she had only packed one book, it had not occurred to her that she might want to read on her honeymoon.

'Shall we dine in here or in the dining-car?' Miles asked.

'Whichever you like.'

'No, you say which you prefer.'

She stared horrified at this polite stranger to whom she had given her life.

'I think the dining-car would be nice.'

Among a crowd of people it might not be so obvious that they had nothing to say to each other.

'You wouldn't rather eat quietly in here?'

'I don't mind a bit if you'd rather.'

'No, you say exactly which you'd rather.'

'I thought it might be a change to stretch our legs walking up to the dining-car. When is the first stop?'

As Indian trains had no corridors one

could only move along them at stations.

'Not for another hour and a half.'

'An hour and a half?' she squeaked, and then repeated her echo in a lower and more normal voice. She did not add 'but what on earth are we going to do for another hour and a half?'

'That's settled then – we'll go to the dining-car. Cigarette?'

Miles sat down opposite her on one of the berths and looked at his watch again. She refused the cigarette. 'Mind if I do?'

'No, no, of course not, go right ahead.'

Miles lay back relaxed in clouds of smoke with his feet up.

'We must get hold of some ponies in the hills,' he told the luggage-rack. 'Do you ride?'

'I'm afraid I never have.'

'I'll teach you.'

Michèle said Miles would be a good teacher, but how long does patience last with a coward?

'Or we might trek up on foot,' he went on.

'I can walk all right. How far is the bungalow from the village?'

'About a mile, they said, but we can send the bearer down for provisions.'

So for three weeks she was to be imprisoned with this handsome, dark stranger beyond any other human aid, since one could not count the bearer who was on

Miles's side anyway.

She saw that it would be foolish to jump out of the train window, but some action was necessary to still a rising panic. She stood up and, as the carriage rattled round a bend, overbalanced into Miles's arms.

'Mind my cigarette,' Miles said, sitting up nervously and feeling around.

'Never mind your silly old cigarette.'

'But it'll set something on fire – did it go in your pocket? Besides, I'd only just started it.'

She found the cigarette in her lap and ground it relentlessly underfoot.

'Too squashed,' she told him firmly. 'Have another, later.'

Miles opened his mouth to complain but she kissed him before he could get a word out.

'Hold on,' he said after a minute, 'what's come over you? This is a new Lucy.'

'I'm married.'

'So you are – or nearly.'

'But soon?'

'But now – darling.'

So they dined in the carriage after all, in dressing-gowns, and finished another bottle of champagne.

PART II

The Honeymoon

Chapter Eight

The little mountain railway dropped them three thousand feet below their destination. With the usual shouts, delays, alarms and inefficiency, their five pieces of luggage were transferred to the taxi which Miles had ordered, and which arrived after only half an hour's wait. It was not a pleasant half-hour, as any hitch in organisation made Miles almost ill. He simply could not get used to the idea of a well-made plan collapsing from the inertia of the other participants. The taxi-driver probably did nothing particular in the half-hour he wasn't there. He may have thought, if he thought about it at all, that the train would be late. Miles stalked up and down the short platform, frustrated by the station's lack of telephone, deaf to Lucy's gentle suggestions about sitting down. From where she sat she could see a wild brown river below, and rocks and dark green jungly trees above going up, up, up the narrow valley on both sides. An enormous brown butterfly alighted on a luggage label beside her in the sun. After two confused nights in the train the earth was undoubtedly moving. She swayed slightly with the wheels of the engine which still clicked on through her.

Miles sulked in the taxi, but with all the horn-blowing and each hair-pin bend which drew them nearer to the top, her heart lifted.

'Oh, Miles, do be happy.'

'I am happy.'

'Look, you can just see the bridge way below us now – help! – that was a close one. I wish he wouldn't take the corners on the precipice side. You aren't happy.'

'Yes – I am.'

'But you aren't smiling. Don't go on being cross about the taxi – we're in it now and everything's all right.'

'I can't grin like an idiot just because I'm going up a mountain.'

'But you're going up a mountain on your honeymoon, that's quite different – and a steady house is so much easier than a train.'

Miles began to worry about the house. She shouldn't have mentioned it.

'We shall be over an hour late now for my appointment with the caretaker – he probably won't have waited.'

'It doesn't matter. We can go down to the village and find him again. We've got three weeks ahead of us.'

'I want to be settled in by nightfall.'

'Of course we shall be – oh, look, a real banana tree.'

In the middle of the village which strad-
dled a high ridge the driver stopped the car
and disappeared. A small crowd, with laughing, copper, Mongolian faces, gathered
round and peered in through the windows.
Miles was not pleased, but this time the
driver came back almost at once with a small
Indian with large glasses and a large green
umbrella who bowed politely and announced himself the caretaker.

'I ride up with you?' he asked. 'It is a con-
venience.'

He sat beside the driver, but turned round
all the time to talk.

'You are now passing magnificent panor-
ama. You will be very happy up there. It is a
happy house. Some people have died, but
what is death? It must come to all of us. I
myself am sixty-five years of age. I am not a
boy, that is why I like to go up on wheels. I
hope I shall be born again a bird. There are
big eagles up there. It is fortunate perhaps
you have no little dog with you. So many
English people like to look after a little dog
and often they disappear in the hills. Go
now more slowly, driver, for the rough road.'

'To whom does the bungalow belong?'
Lucy asked.

'To Jenkins Sahib, in Calcutta. He comes
up in the summer-time to leave his wife and
children, but in the spring he does not come.
Then he makes a *bunderbust* with Agency for

127

letting. He is not often successful. This is a lucky year. You are a lucky lady, I can see that.' He bowed to her again.

'Do you think he wants his palm crossed with silver?' Miles asked in French. She was furious, and pretended she had not heard.

'Which people died?' she asked.

'Many people die. It is a terrible war-time, we hear bad stories even here – so many widows and little children.'

'Oh, I thought you meant somebody died at the bungalow.'

'No – no – why should you think that? It is a very happy bungalow, nobody dies there. English people who feel like dying go in hospital for that, and Indians go back to their families. It is not possible anybody dies in Jenkins Sahib's bungalow. There now it is. Ah, it is gone.'

For some minutes the road twisted round under the bungalow, which came and went as the car turned. Then suddenly they were on top of it, down a short drive. The caretaker sprang out and scrambled up the steps to the veranda, where he turned and cried:

'Welcome – welcome! You are now at home.' He clapped his hands and five servants appeared.

'They will look after you – they are all good boys.'

But Lucy had looked behind and seen the garden ending with a tangled rose bush and a steep drop and, far, far away across the valley, folded brown hills, soft blue hills, and floating high above them all a jagged line of apricot snow. 'Oh, Miles! Can we see Everest?'

The caretaker struggled with a wish to give them everything they wanted, but admitted in the end that Kanchenjunga was the best he could manage.

It was dark indoors after the shining garden, but not too dark for her to see a shrouded three-piece suite and the dusty surfaces of other more exposed bits of furniture.

'Have the servants been here long?'

'They came yesterday to make all ready for you. Pray be seated.'

She sat cautiously on the edge of one of the dust-sheets.

'The *mem-sahib* had these white covers made for visitors. It is very good. You sit on this and then when Jenkins Sahib comes we lift all off and, up Jenkins, all is clean and unspoilt below.'

'Oh.'

Perhaps they would spend a lot of time in bed, and the rest of it on horseback. They need never sit in here at all. But she had forgotten Miles was not so accommodating.

'It won't do, I'm afraid. This isn't good enough for my wife.'

'I don't mind, Miles, really.'

'Get the servants busy and have the room properly done out in an hour. All the dust-sheets off.'

'But it is so practical like this–' the caretaker wailed.

'All the dust-sheets off,' Miles repeated louder. 'And a good fire lit, and what arrangements have you made about dinner?'

'We await the *mem-sahib's* orders.'

'Send the cook in at once.'

The caretaker shuffled out, all the gentle kindness wiped off his face. Miles walked up and down again just as he had done on the platform below. She looked out of the window and tried to keep her mind on the distant mountains.

Miles ordered chicken and salad and bread and butter and fruit and coffee and milk and eggs and bacon, and more, while the cook waited, hands together, nodding his head for each item.

'Go *now* to the village,' he finished. The cook went. The caretaker had returned and stood anxiously just inside the door.

'Now for the bedroom,' Miles said briskly.

'If beds stood in here, how pleasant to watch firelight dancing–' the caretaker began hopefully, with his eyes on the ceiling, but Miles paid no attention to that sort of nonsense. He strode out of the room and began opening doors off the hall. The first was a cupboard, the second a bathroom and the third a bedroom. The door had clearly not been opened since last September, or whenever Jenkins Sahib left for Calcutta. The room breathed a rich smell of moist gloom.

'I suppose it snows up here in the winter,' Miles said flinging open the shutters. The mountains were again in the house. She turned her back on the damp beds and leaned on the window-sill in the sun. Miles was giving more orders about fires and blankets and hot-water-bottles. Presently she swung her legs out and slipped down into the garden, and wandered along the weedy, overgrown paths till she came to a wooden seat behind a scented hedge facing the valley and the mountain.

She heard Miles calling, but kept quiet. He came round the corner of her secret hedge.

'There you are. Didn't you hear me?'

'Yes – I did, really.'

'Why didn't you answer?' he looked puzzled rather than angry, but it was still impossible to explain she had wanted to hide from him.

'Have you settled everything?' she asked.

'More or less. You ought to be doing it really – all this household stuff.'

'Oh, please – surely I needn't learn now? We shan't ever have a proper house in India and certainly not in Burma, and daily helps in England will be so different. I'll learn

131

then, honestly.'

'I'm sorry about all this. I meant it to be perfect for you when we arrived.'

'Darling, don't worry. I love it. I didn't believe it could be so perfect. Just look in front of you.'

'Yes, but the beds are soaking. I doubt if they'll get them dry by tonight.'

'Miles, I don't *care*.'

'You'll care soon enough if you're crippled with rheumatoid arthritis.'

'I shall expect you to cure me instantly.'

'Can't.'

'Well, if the beds aren't dry, we'll sleep on the sofa.'

'What – both of us?'

'Anyway, let's not think about it yet. Something may turn up.'

'I hope supper is going to turn up all right.'

'Where are you off to now?'

'Looking to see if there's any sign of the cook on the road.'

'He can't get back yet with all the orders you gave him. Do relax. Could we have a drink?'

'Why not? Out here?'

'Yes – then we shan't be in the way of the dusting.'

The drink was a good idea. Miles fetched a bottle and found two glasses and was reassured by the busyness of the servants.

They sat a long time in the garden and returned to find the sitting-room transformed with hideous lupin chintz and a blazing wood fire. There was even a distant smell of slightly-cooking chicken.

'You see?' She crouched in front of the fire admiring the flames. 'Everything really is all right.'

But Miles went off to the bedroom and came back to say the fire in there was smoking badly and the beds as damp as ever. All the effects of two gins were wasted.

'But it doesn't matter.'

'It does. We can't spend the first night of our honeymoon on a sofa.'

'But it isn't the first night. It's the third.'

'You can hardly count two nights in a train.'

It was a pity they had not counted. They had not been a success, that was her fault, but they had surely counted as experience. Her heart sank, she wanted no more new beginnings.

After supper the servants withdrew to their own quarters. Miles and Lucy, alone with an uncertain oil lamp and the sinking fire, sat in a silence broken only by Miles's frequent visits to examine the blankets, which involved banging two doors twice.

At eleven o'clock he pronounced the situation hopeless.

'We'll be up all night if we wait for the

beds to dry.'

'I'm tired enough to sleep anywhere. I'll have the floor.'

'No. I can't allow that. You have the sofa.'

'No – you have it.'

They squabbled politely for five minutes and finally drew lots. She got the floor, but as a consolation prize she also had both bedding rolls from the train.

They lay down fully dressed and in a few minutes Miles was snoring. Lucy waited stiffly for sleep to fall. Nothing happened. A small intimate draught blew in under the door off the far-away snows and snuggled down her back. The fire no longer gave out any heat, she heard a distant howling (of wolves?) and began to wonder who had been murdered in this room. The caretaker had been too eager to get away from the subject of death after his slip. She laid her coat along the floor by the door, but when she had struggled down into the sleeping-bag the draught was still with her.

She tried the windows next and found behind the thick curtains one open. She pulled it shut and tried to sleep again, but the draught now seemed more persistent than ever. She thought she saw a blue glow in the room over by the window. She could bear it no longer and threw herself on top of Miles in desperation. Miles woke fighting the enemy off, when he opened his eyes he stopped hitting her.

'Oh, Miles, there's a ghost!'

'Nonsense – where?'

'Over there by the window – a blue one. I heard it howling.'

'Lucy, have you gone off your head?'

'Not yet, but I'm so frightened, darling, do *do* something.'

'But I can't see anything or hear anything, and if I did I wouldn't know what to attack ghosts with. Do be calm. Shall I light the lamp?'

'You'll never find it in the dark.'

'Of course I shall. It's just over there.'

'Don't go. Don't leave me alone.'

'Stop being hysterical. I'm only going three yards.'

'I'm coming too.'

She clung to his arm as he groped his way across the room. He stubbed his toe twice and knocked over a small table breaking a glass full of water.

'Don't move now, Lucy. You'll get glass in your feet.'

'I don't care.'

'Lucy, do as I say. Stand still.'

'I can't.'

'Control yourself.'

'How?'

'As soon as I get this lamp on I'll show you how.'

He lit a couple of matches and the lamp

flared up to make a wide black mark on the ceiling. He fiddled it back to normal and turned to her.

'Now what's all this about ghosts?'

'Over there it was – by the curtain.'

They both looked at the gap in the curtain through which even against the lamp the moonlight streamed. Miles walked over and jerked the curtains apart so that the whole of the blue jar on the sideboard was luminous. He did not say anything.

'Sorry, Miles.'

'Anything else worrying you?'

'Well, only the howling, and I expect it was a jackal.'

'Shall we get some sleep then?'

'Yes, please.'

'Would you be more comfortable on the sofa?'

'No, I'm all right on the floor, thank you, really.'

He turned out the light and they lay down again. The tears trickled out of the corners of her eyes and down into her ears. She moved her head restlessly.

'Lucy?'

'M'm'

'You still awake?'

'No.'

'What's the matter?'

'Nothing.'

'You're crying.'

'No, I'm not.'

'Look, Lucy, you mustn't *mind so* much.'

'I don't.'

'I know I'm quick-tempered, but I don't really mean it.'

'Of course not.'

'Lucy, where are you? Is that your face? It's wet. Darling, you *are* crying.'

'Leave me alone.'

She rolled over and buried her head in the lupin cushion she was using as a pillow. It smelt frowsty and unfriendly. But Miles was kneeling beside her and pulled her into his arms.

'Look, sweetheart, do please let's get some sleep now.'

'I'm not stopping you.'

'Yes, you are. I can't go to sleep to the sound of muffled gulping.'

'Miles, you don't love me at all,' she burst out. 'I can't think why you married me. I wish I was dead.' Her voice rose miserably. Miles shifted into a more comfortable position on the floor with his back to the sofa.

'Now listen, darling. You need some sleep too. You're imagining things.'

'But you don't say it.'

'Say what?'

'Say you love me – even in the train you didn't.'

'Didn't I? You probably didn't hear through

137

the noise of the engine.'

'And you're tired of me already. It's the third night and you don't want me. I know I'm no good, but how am I going to learn otherwise?'

Miles sighed, and began again as patiently as he could:

'I'm just tired, full stop. Not tired of you. How could I be when we've hardly started?'

'Just because of.'

'Because of what?'

'Because of hardly starting. We probably never shall start and it'll be all my fault.'

'Lucy, let's go to sleep now and discuss it in the morning.'

'You might just as well begin the divorce right away.'

'But we're too tired to make sense, either of us. All my plans went wrong, but it'll be different tomorrow.'

'Nothing will be different, we'll still be us.'

'Yes, but not such exhausted us. Come on, there's a good girl. Give me a kiss and call it a day.'

He touched her forehead in the dark, but she dragged his mouth down and felt him come alive.

And in the morning, of course, everything was different. The sun flooded the house and set the dust sparkling. The house-boy brought really hot shaving water for Miles, and the cook made good coffee for breakfast. She was stiff from lying on the floor, but wonderfully cheerful. Miles could not read the paper as there was no paper, but even this did not upset him. After breakfast he suggested riding.

'Not *today*.'

'Why not?'

'I'm so stiff already.'

'It'll shake you straight again.'

'But, Miles, it's another thing I'm not good at. I can't learn two things at once.'

'Of course you can. We'll go very slowly.'

He would not listen to any objections and by eleven o'clock the animals were champing at the door. The word 'pony' had given her a vivid picture of a small, shaggy thing with very short legs so that one could brake by putting a foot down. These two ferocious ponies looked indistinguishable from ordinary mettlesome horses, and somewhat higher.

'Miles, I'll never even get *on*, all the way up there.'

'I'll give you a hand up. Here – one two and over she goes.'

'Now I shall fall straight off. There's nothing to hang on by. It's ears aren't long enough. Oh, darling, please, must I?'

'Take the reins, silly girl. Now watch me.'

'Please, can the man come too and hold its horrible head?'

'No, of course not. Now follow me. I

promise we won't go fast.'

Her horse had started to walk after the other, so she was forced to follow as she had no idea how to stop; she clenched her teeth and clung on, relieved to see that Miles was riding uphill. Miles looked very strong, straight and purposeful from the back. In the comfort of Harley Street he might even grow stout, in Harley Street they would be rich. A competent housekeeper would manage everything while she had a fine time, and lovely clothes, and maybe a few beautiful and intelligent children. After last night a divorce seemed unlikely. Thinking about last night she fell off her horse for the first time. It was not a painful fall, more of a subsidence. Her horse, Miles's horse, and Miles, paid no attention. Both horses continued to pick their way carefully upwards. Miles did not look round as she joined the walkers. It was stony on foot but she felt safer.

Unfortunately her peace ended ten minutes later when Miles noticed the empty horse. He waited patiently for the horse and, later, Lucy, to catch up.

'Why didn't you shout?'

'I was all right. It didn't hurt.'

'I'll help you up again.'

'I really prefer to walk.'

'Don't be silly. We're coming to an open grassy bit where we can have a good gallop.'

'I'd rather gallop about without the horse.'

'Lucy, you aren't trying. Come on.' He hitched the two horses to a tree and walked towards her.

'I'm not getting on that horse again.' She backed away.

'Yes, you are – if I have to carry you.'

'It doesn't like me. I know it doesn't. It keeps putting its head round and leering.'

'Lucy, come here.'

'Shan't – come and catch me.'

She scrambled across some rocks and dropped down on the other side to find a hidden grassy ledge. She could hear Miles blundering after her, but he went round the wrong way and fetched up below. She leaned over and hit him coyly on the head with a bunch of yellow rock roses.

He pulled himself up beside her.

'Now, are you coming riding?'

'No, I don't like riding.'

'You are going to learn to like it. It's good for you.'

'It's not good for anyone to be scared out of their wits.'

'You can't be truly scared of a poor old beast that would die of heart failure if it got up any speed.'

'You mentioned gallops.'

'Figure of speech – come on, darling.'

'No, it's so warm and soft here. Had you noticed we are lying on a bank of thyme?'

'I thought something smelled good. You are demoralising me – in the middle of the morning.'

'It's a quarter to afternoon by your watch. Miles, I love you.'

'So you should. This would be very unsuitable otherwise.'

'But you still haven't said–'

'Nothing needs saying any more.'

Behind his head, she could see a huge bird hovering over the valley.

'Darling, is that a hawk or an eagle?'

'Where?'

'Across there.'

'I can't turn round. I'm too comfortable. What does it look like?'

'It's a long way away – golden brown with wide, wide wings.'

'Sounds interesting. I get a better view of the thyme from here.'

'Funny to feel on top of the world, on top of the world. Darling, you *are* clever.'

'So are you.'

'I love you more than ever, Miles.'

'It's very bad for me.'

'Why?'

'Gives me a swelled head.'

'You certainly look a bit smug.'

'I'm not – just dropping of. You know we still haven't had enough sleep on this honeymoon. Tonight we'll go to bed in the real

142

aired beds immediately after supper.'

'Lovely,' she whispered, shutting her eyes against the green and black sun.

But late that night she was still awake.

'Tell me about being a doctor, Miles.'

'Now?'

'Why not?'

'I'm nearly asleep. I'll tell you in the morning.'

'But it's so much easier to talk in the dark.'

'Not if you are as sleepy as I am.'

'Oh, please–'

'Well, it's like being anything else once it's your job. Jolly hard work with rewarding moments. Now close your eyes.'

'They are closed. I'm trying to see you with a big black car and a small black bag. Do you think I'll be a good doctor's wife?'

'Hopeless, I imagine. Good night.'

'Oh, darling, why do you say that? Why should I be hopeless? I'll try terribly hard and always have a shepherd's pie keeping hot for you. Oh, Miles, don't go to sleep. Miles–'

But she was answered by a gentle snoring, either feigned or real, and left to fret on by herself about the future.

Chapter Nine

As soon as he woke up in the morning, she tried again:

'Darling, did you mean that last night?'

Miles rubbed his eyes and rolled over to sip his chilling tea.

'Mean what?'

'What you said about me being hopeless.'

'What did I say about you being hopeless? This tea's cold.'

'Oh, you must remember – it was a horrid thing to say. About me as a hopeless wife.'

'I'm sure I didn't say that. You're doing quite well as a wife so far. Is that all the sugar he brought in?'

'No – a doctor's wife. Because I can answer telephones like anything and I can soon learn to cook. I can cook dull things anyway because I did at Rachel's so it shouldn't take long to advance to *cordon bleu* stuff.'

'Did you do all the cooking at Rachel's?'

'No, we took it in turns, except Rachel.'

'Why not Rachel?'

'She was out too often, and in any case it was her house so she provided the shelter and we did the housework.'

'I can't imagine Rachel doing housework.'

He lay back with his hands behind his head on the pillow, looking up at a crack in the ceiling.

'Neither can I. But I suppose she tries a bit now, for Henry.'

Miles stopped smiling and looked across at her.

'I don't know why you think it will be difficult to be a doctor's wife.'

'I don't. I thought I could do it easily. It was you who said I'd be hopeless.'

'Oh, forget it, Lucy. You take everything too seriously. What shall we do today? Go riding? Is it another fine day?'

She slipped out and pulled the curtains right back. The sun seized her all over.

'Lucy,' Miles called, 'dressing-gown. Don't forget the servants.'

She came back obediently and buttoned herself in.

'Couldn't we send the servants away?'

'Whatever for?'

'So that we could have the house to ourselves and I could look after you.'

'No, thank you – time enough for that when I *have* to put up with your ministrations.'

'Oh, Miles, you're going to say it again.'

'Say what?'

'That I'm no good.'

'No, I'm not. I only mean we may as well have comfort while we can get it and since I

145

put the fear of God into the servants they haven't been doing too badly. Now, as I said before, what shall we do today?'

'Need we do anything?'

'Of course we must do something.'

'We could sit in the sun and read, or go for a little walk.'

'No, I think we'll go down to the Club and have a game of tennis.'

'But I don't like tennis.'

'Of course you do – all nice English girls like tennis.'

'I don't. I can't hit the ball. I can't even see it coming over the net.'

'You must need glasses, better get your eyes tested.'

'They were – last year. They're perfectly all right. I just get nervous.'

'Then you must go to a psychiatrist.'

'Oh, Miles, just because I don't like tennis?'

He walked into the bathroom to shave and shouted back:

'There seem to be rather a lot of ordinary things that make you nervous, and extraordinary things that *should*, which don't.'

'Well, anyway,' she shouted too, 'I can't go to a psychiatrist up here so you'll just have to take me as I am for the time being.'

'Very cuddlesome too,' Miles said through his toothbrush.

That sounded better so she pulled on her

dress saying:

'No tennis, then.'

Miles came back into the bedroom with a towel round his neck.

'Better light in here,' he explained to the looking-glass. 'Let's go down to the Club and I'll find someone to give me a knock-up and you can have a pow-wow with the ladies.'

'A what?'

'Pow-wow – chinwag – chat.'

'Yes – yes, I heard you the first time, I just couldn't believe my ears. You were being funny, weren't you?'

'I expect so. I don't make many jokes, so you can usually see one coming a mile off. You look sweet in blue.'

'Thank you. Do you think your mother will like me?'

'Of course she will – she'll like anyone I tell her to. What made you suddenly think of her?'

'Blue.'

'Blue?'

'Yes – mothers always like girls to wear blue.'

'Do they? I wouldn't know, without sisters.'

'And I wouldn't really know, without a mother or sisters, but I've heard tell. Anyway, she's quite happy and independent in that Kensington flat, isn't she?'

'Mother? Good Lord, yes – don't start

147

worrying about her. She's never interfered with me and she's not likely to start now.'

'You don't think she'll be offended, us getting married without her there?'

'But she couldn't possibly come out to India with a war on.'

'No, but perhaps it would have been more sensible for us to have waited?'

His denial was not as passionate as she'd hoped:

'Might have been more sensible–' but then he added, 'not such fun, though.'

'Oh, darling–' She flung herself at him. 'As long as it's fun for you–'

'Hey – mind the razor. Now I've cut myself.'

'I'm so sorry. Goodness, it's bleeding. What shall I do?'

'Pass me a piece of cotton-wool.'

'Oughtn't you to put some Dettol on or something in case the razor was rusty?'

'Have we got any Dettol?'

'No.'

'Then I can't.'

'What is it people use for snake bites?'

'Potassium permanganate.'

'Shall I see if they've got any of that in the kitchen?'

'They won't have. Do stop fussing. I'm quite all right. Besides, I don't use rusty razors.'

In spite of Miles's suggestion, she didn't

have a pow-wow with the *mem-sahibs* at the Club. She couldn't see one unattended anyway, so she took *Persuasion* over to a shady grass bank not far from Miles's tennis court, and with the soothing twang of the racquets in her ears presently fell asleep.

Miles shook her awake a little roughly.

'Finished your game, darling?' she asked fondly.

'Yes, thanks. Why didn't you sit with the others on the terrace?'

'I wanted to be near you.'

He looked taller than ever standing over her.

'You've got grass stains on your dress. There wasn't much point in being near me if you went to sleep. You do have a genius for making yourself conspicuous.'

'Surely nobody noticed me asleep out here?'

'Of course they did. Everyone knows we are on our honeymoon.'

'What difference does that make?'

'Oh well, if you can't see, never mind. Come and have a drink.'

'Is it time?'

'After midday.'

He moved away without holding his hand out to her and she ran after him.

'If they are interested in our honeymoon you'd better try and look loving,' she pointed out.

Miles only scowled. 'Did you brush your hair this morning?'

'Of course. What's the matter with it?'

'Full of grass and all on end.'

'I was reading first.'

'Does that make your hair stand on end?'

'Pushing my hand into it does.'

'You've got too many nervous gestures, Lucy.'

'You're a nice one to talk – a bundle of nervous irritation. Anyone would think you were frustrated.'

She put her hand to her mouth, but it was too late. Miles gave one hating look, and then turned his back and walked away from the Club and out on to the road again. She hesitated for a few minutes. She would have liked a drink of orange juice, but she didn't feel strong enough to face the bar alone now she knew she was an object of interest. How many of the eyes on the terrace had taken in their horrid scene? She shook the grass out of her hair and followed Miles slowly up the hill towards home.

Miles didn't look behind him once, and as he reached the bungalow and walked stiffly down the drive out of sight she knew she couldn't bear to go in and start the row straight away. She climbed on, up the rough track they had taken with the horses, past red and purple rhododendrons. When the trees ended she left the path and scrambled

150

up the rocks to the ledge where they had lain. She lay down and pressed her face into the warm thyme. Miles would be sitting alone at the lunch table, glaring at curry and lager, but probably managing to eat up bravely.

She stayed there all the long afternoon in the sun, waiting for him to come. When it began to grow dark she realised she would have to be the first to apologise. The sun had disappeared suddenly behind a sharp peak on the other side of the valley and left her in cold grey shadow. She went slowly home with a blister coming up on her heel, falling over stones in the half-light with the weight of her heart to carry.

The living-room lamp shone out across the drive, she walked up to the window and looked in. The room was empty. She imagined Miles taking a bath before supper, but found the bedroom and the bathroom in darkness. She stood by the fire warming her hands and called out to the servants. The house-boy came in and told her Miles had gone down to the Club.

'How long ago?'

The boy did not know.

'When did he say he would come back?'

He did not say.

'No message for me?'

None.

She ordered a bath and supper. She was

cold and very hungry. She ate off a tray by the fire in her dressing-gown with hair lying damp on her neck. Later she put her feet up on the sofa. Miles didn't arrive till well after ten o'clock, in a taxi. She composed a reproachful face and waited. She could hear him arguing with the driver, then he slammed the front door and came in.

'So you've decided to return?' he sounded aggressive.

'I could say the same to you. Have you had supper?'

'Yes, thank you. I wasn't going to eat alone up here.'

'I was in by half-past seven.'

'About time too.'

'Were you worried?'

'No, why should I be? I guessed where you were. I thought you'd come in when it got uncomfortable.'

This stranger wasn't even polite and smelt of whisky.

'Oh, Miles, you've been drinking.'

'Any objections?'

'Yes – lots–'

'Well, don't voice them. If I feel like a couple of drinks I shall take a couple of drinks. You aren't my keeper.'

'It must have been much more than a couple to make you so cross.'

'Don't nag.'

'I wasn't – simply stating a fact. And I

don't see why you have to get drunk just because I spent the afternoon up the hill.'

'And the morning making a fool of me.'

'You made a fool of me. It was you who walked out on me at the Club.'

'That's beside the point.'

'Oh, darling, please, what point? There isn't a point – it's all awful.'

'Whose fault is that?'

'Oh, mine – mine – mine. I don't care but I can't bear you looking at me like that. We were so happy yesterday. I thought everything was going to be all right.'

'Looking at you like what?'

'As if you loathed me.'

'Of course I don't loathe you.'

'Don't look loathing then.'

'I can't help it. My face is made sinister.'

'It isn't – it's a delicious face and it often looks as kind and open as a sunflower.'

'Sunflowers have black hearts.'

'Miles, please, come here where I can touch you.'

'No, then we shall get confused.'

'But we are hopelessly confused now. Wouldn't it be better to be pleasantly confused?'

'No, we must get this straight.'

'Get what straight?'

'Whatever it was we were talking about.'

'But we weren't.'

'We must have been – my ears are shuddering with words.'

'Please kiss me.'

'Lucy, you seem to think kissing is the answer to everything.'

'But it is. I've learnt that much anyway. Please.'

He came and stood at the end of the sofa. She twisted round and pulled him down beside her, but he sat straight upright, unrelenting.

'Oh, darling, look at me.'

'I can't. You'll say I look loathing again.'

'No, I shan't. I'm sure I could change it to loving if you'd only try a bit too.'

But he yawned and rubbed his hand over his eyes.

'It's no good, Lucy. You'd better leave me alone tonight.'

'Why?'

'You noticed yourself I'd been drinking.'

'But if you tried to get cheerful again I'm sure you could.'

'For God's sake, Lucy, don't bother me.'

She drew back, but he saw her bleak face.

'I'm sorry – did that sound very harsh? I'm not fit company for anyone tonight.'

'Why did you have to go and spoil things, Miles?'

'Nothing is spoilt except this evening and this afternoon. Now please let me go to bed in peace.'

'Shall I undress you?'

'I'm only bad-tempered, not incapable, thank you.'

'Miles, will this happen often?'

'That depends on you.'

'I mean, did you always drink a lot without my knowing?'

'Not as a rule.'

'Then it's all my fault?'

'So far.'

'It *can't* be – you aren't being fair.'

'No, I don't suppose I am. Alcohol gives one prejudices.'

He stood up and walked out and into the bedroom, she followed close behind, thinking he might fall. He sat down on one of the beds and fumbled with his shoe-laces. She knelt beside him and untied them but he only said:

'I'd rather be alone, thanks.'

'But this is my room too.'

'Can't you wait till I've finished?'

So she trailed back into the sitting-room and sat huddled up in a chair until the noises of running water and dropping of shoes and clothes had died away. By the time she crawled into her own bed Miles was asleep with his mouth open.

He was sorry in the sunlight.

'I must have been hell last night, darling.'

'You certainly were.'

'Have you been up for hours?'

155

'Hours.'

She moved across the rug to make room for him. She was lying in the sunny garden with her eyes shut.

'Why didn't you wake me?'

'Thought you might be annoyed.'

'Oh dear, oh dear. It must be even worse than I remembered. Lucy, open your lovely, lucid, limpid eyes and tell me I'm forgiven.'

'Don't see why I should.' But she opened them grudgingly and could not withstand his laughter. She laughed too.

'That's better.' Miles relaxed and lay down beside her. 'Can't think why I haven't a hangover – must be the mountain air. Do you know who I met in the Club?'

'No. Who?'

'Chap called Turner I spent six months with in Iceland.'

'That must have been very amusing.'

'It was – we had a hell of an evening.'

'I know.'

'I mean it. He knew everybody. Been up here for three weeks. I said we'd lunch with him today.'

'How did you explain my absence last night?'

'Said you'd gone to bed early with a head-ache.'

'Leaving out the word "early" I suppose it was more or less true. What time are we lunching?'

156

'Twelve forty-five.'

'It's after twelve now.'

'Go and make yourself ever so beautiful so that I can be proud of you.'

'Aren't you proud of me untidy?'

'Of course not. Why should I be?'

'I thought you might love me whatever my hair looked like.'

'I want my wife to be a credit to me.'

'In that case I shall have to sleep in curlers.'

'Nonsense. Clever women manage without that. Rachel never–'

'–never slept in curlers?'

'Oh damn!' Miles said, rolling over on his face. There was a long silence. A butterfly poised on the toe of her red sandal. One is never prepared for the pompous moments. She shook her foot and the butterfly slipped away to the sweet peas.

'Miles – listen – it doesn't matter, honestly. I knew.'

'How did you know? Rachel never said, did she?'

Rachel never said – Rachel who betrayed everyone to everyone else in the sweetest possible way – Rachel who had informed them all at breakfast, half-awake in their dressing-gowns over the fried bread, that she wouldn't be home for a week as she was going to Devonshire to spend a wonderful leave with Miles – and when she returned radiant, had not spared any loving details:

'He's so strong – it's not what he says, but the way he looks. I thought I'd melt with happiness – and do you know, such a funny thing happened. We were playing all the normal rules, of course, rings and signing on as Mrs. Spender and not more than three days in each hotel because of ration books. It wasn't far from his unit and he didn't want to get into trouble so we kept pretty quiet and just went out for long walks and bathed and tried not to attract attention, and then on the last night what *do* you think happened?'

'What?' asked Priscilla and Lucy, Lucy longing with agony to know, and Priscilla just to humour Rachel whom she dearly loved, but who was interrupting her air-graph to Allan.

'Well,' Rachel looked at them both, her eyes shining. 'Miles got up and took down the black-out and opened the window – he hadn't anything on, of course.'

'Of course,' Lucy said, trying to bear the idea with fortitude.

'And he gave the window a gentle push and it just fell right out on to a conveniently placed pile of flower-pots below. You never heard such a crash. You should have seen his face with his empty hand still sticking out into the garden.'

'So the manager came and there was a row?'

'Not exactly a row. Miles dashed into his

158

pyjamas and paid for the damage at once, and I got down under the bedclothes and tried not to let them see me giggling, but there's no doubt we were *noticed*, if you see what I mean.'

Lucy did not see how anyone could avoid noticing Rachel and her starry hair at any time, let alone Miles with his fierce, dark, unfair good looks. Together they must have been enough to stop a circus.

She banished Rachel and put her hand lightly on Miles's arm.

'Did she?' Miles asked again, not lifting his face.

'You don't have to be told that sort of thing. If you love somebody, you just know.'

'It was a long time ago.' There was an ache in his voice. Longing or regret?

'I know.' She kept her own voice calm and resolute, feeling older every second. 'That's all over and we can forget about it. It's the future that matters.' Who's this talking?

Miles put his hand out and held hers then, so she knew she'd managed all right so far.

'You're a wonderful girl, what should I do without you?'

'You aren't without me yet, so don't let's worry and meanwhile I must go and change for this Turner.'

She patted his hand briskly and walked into the house.

159

Turner was a dear old bore with a healthy moustache, or maybe just she never was in Iceland. She had no contribution to make beyond some incorrect facts about sphagnum moss. After several drinks and a heavy lunch she was in terror of dozing off again in a basket chair on the terrace while Miles and Turner recalled old binges, when somebody twitched her hair sharply from behind She gave a shrill screech, and turned to see Steve McMahon.

'It's the girl I knocked about,' Steve yelled at the top of his voice. Everyone who wasn't already looking at her because of the scream turned to look now. Steve pulled her to her feet to make it even easier for about thirty people to see her properly.

'What about a kiss?' he added, 'for old times' sake, and how's our dear Aunt Gertie keeping?'

He kissed her quickly, and too intimately, while she was still staring at him, flabbergasted, and began to drag her over towards the bar saying: 'What'll you have – a burra peg with me?'

'My husband–' she finally managed to gasp in a faint voice, digging her toes in too late half-way across the floor.

'Your *what?*' Steve roared, as if she'd said she kept a crocodile.

'My husband – Miles – I want you to meet – Steve,' she tried with a waved arm to close

160

the awkward gap between them.

'I'd remember him anywhere with his black scowl,' Steve said admiringly. Miles was standing now too, with eyebrows drawn for battle.

'Lucy, my darling, why did you betray me? You promised to wait for me till the cows came home in Killarney.'

'Oh, Steve – please don't. You know I never–'

'Those were your very words treasured to this day. "I'll wait for you, Steve," you said, "for the sake of your black eyes and your terrible brogue," and what do I find you doing the very next time we meet but honey-mooning with another. It's more than mortal flesh can stand.'

'Let's have some whisky then,' she suggested in desperation.

'Miles,' she added, 'this is my cousin Steve McMahon, you know – Aunt Gertie's nephew, the one who was bought out of the firm and shipped overseas, but he's quite harmless really.'

Miles unscrambled his eyebrows slowly.

'I didn't know you had an Aunt Gertie?'

'Didn't you? There are so many when it comes to the count.'

The interest round them gradually died down as Steve was only a relation.

'And what, may I ask, are you doing on my honeymoon?'

'On my way to have a stab at Tibet.'

'Surely they haven't got a war on there?'

'Not yet – but they will have one day and I'd like to see it first.'

'You'll never get in, and you'll miss an important campaign here.'

'No fear – I'll be in Burma by the time they take Rangoon.'

'Your eyes aren't black anyway.'

'Neither are yours.'

'We weren't talking about me.'

'Who wasn't?'

'Oh, Steve, do be sensible for a minute.'

'Why? I have to keep up a grinning façade to protect my wounded heart. Do you think they can hear us?'

Miles and Turner were standing only a few feet away with fresh drinks, but they were back in Reykjavik in spirit.

'It doesn't matter if they do. I have no secrets from my husband.'

'You may not have, but he's such a big bullying brute that I'd hesitate to make love to his adorable little wife with himself with his ears cocked. Why *didn't* you wait?'

'You never asked me to. You didn't even give me an address.'

'What an oversight. What was I thinking of? Would you have?'

'No – of course not. I hardly know you.'

'Kindred spirits don't have to know each other long in time.'

'Where will you be in Burma?'

'All over – in the summer.'

'I'm going – with a canteen force.'

'That's the girl. We'll paint the Shwe Dâgon red together. What are you going to do with Ivan the Terrible?'

'Who?'

'This husband you've got yourself mixed up with.'

'He's going to Burma too.'

'Pity.'

Steve lit another cigarette and started on another whisky. Miles and Turner decided to make the talk general, so the three men covered the Burmese campaign pretty thoroughly, considering only one of them had ever been east of Assam, and she fought her falling eyelids. It ended with Miles inviting Steve and Turner up to dinner later at the bungalow.

Turner arrived early, while she was having a bath, and Miles stuck his head through the window to tell her they would walk up to the end of the lane to see the view and she was to follow when dressed. She made a more or less assenting noise and lay back to think peacefully in the steam until she heard the scrunching of one person on the gravel and guessed that Steve had come. She walked into the bedroom wrapped in a large pink bath-towel to find him standing there looking at her yellow dress laid out on the bed.

'Not the colour for you now, surely?' he said.

'What are you doing here?'

'No door-bell. Never have got used to shouting for servants. Tried empty sitting-room first. Why yellow?'

'I used to have it. It's a dress I've had a long time and I'm fond of.'

'When you were dark and twice as charming.'

'Don't you like blondes?'

'Oh yes – the real ones.'

'Don't I look convincing like this?'

'Hardly, to anyone tall enough to look down on the top of your head.'

He came and stood over her to demonstrate his point. Her head came to his shoulder.

'You see,' he said, touching her hair, 'telltale roots – black as a starling's wing.'

'You're too thin anyway,' she said furiously. 'And I don't know you, and get out of my room. Miles will be in any minute and have a fit.'

'No, he won't. I watched him out of sight up the hill before I arrived. Fine strong back and legs he has. I don't wonder you fell for him.'

'Steve, will you get out or have I got to call the servants to put you out?'

'You wouldn't dare call, and they wouldn't

dare touch a *sahib*.'

'They'd touch a *sahib* who was insulting a *mem-sahib* all right.'

'Now be reasonable, my darling, where's the insult in saying you were twice as charming in your natural state when you're already fit to kill dyed up as you are?'

He lit a cigarette and lay down on one of the beds. She snatched her dress and went back into the bathroom without another word. She took a long time over her face, but he was still there when she came out, blowing smoke rings at the ceiling. As she slipped into her evening shoes and sat down to brush her hair Miles walked into the room saying: 'Come on, darling, you *must* be ready by now,' before he saw Steve dropping ash on his pillow. Steve swung his legs round slowly, without any guilty haste, and she watched in the looking-glass Miles mastering his annoyance.

'Been here long?' he asked.

'About half an hour,' Steve answered.

'Why didn't you give him a drink, Lucy?'

'I was in the bath.'

She shouldn't have said that, but Miles still controlled himself.

'Come on, McMahon,' he said shortly. 'Have a drink now.'

Steve ambled after him, blowing a kiss to her reflection.

165

The row came when the guests had gone. She was expecting it and hurried quickly into bed, where she felt safer, while Miles was still seeing them to the end of the drive. She even pretended to be asleep, but Miles wouldn't allow that escape. He sat down on the bed and shook her shoulder.

'Now listen, Lucy, it's all very well that chap being your cousin, but that doesn't give him any right to watch you dress.'

'He didn't.'

'He was in here when I came back and he'd obviously been here for ages.'

'I dressed in the bathroom. Oh, what does it matter, darling – it's such a little thing.'

'It's not little to me. Now you're my wife I want everything about you to be mine. I don't even want other people to see you brushing your hair.'

'Miles, do be reasonable. That's the most public act.'

'Well – it shouldn't be and I don't want it to happen again.'

'Do you think you've got any right to talk to me like that? You know I'm not like–'

'For Christ's sake, you're not going to hold that against me for the rest of our lives? We're living in the twentieth century.'

'Don't you understand that I love you?'

He held her face in both his hands and stared at her.

'I believe you,' he said softly and began to

kiss her slowly, deeply, but without another word.

And if he is killed, what to remember? The word so long outlasts the flesh and if there are no words and the flesh is rotten. This cruel, angry talking will grind over and over through lonely nights till I long for maggots in the mind.

She kissed him desperately trying to drag hope from his live and silent tongue. Hope for her, hope for them. Would he love me more if I loved him less? I must not say it again – not ask – not long for assurance.

'Miles, don't get killed – promise me.'

'Of course I shan't, darling. They don't put doctors in the front line.'

'You never know, all those horrible fox-holes – and with the Japanese the front line is changeable. Sometimes it's at the back.'

'I'm sure they won't get me, anyway.'

'I wish I could be as confident.'

'Darling, you are supposed to support and encourage me.'

'I can't. I don't feel brave about anything. How could I manage without you?'

'You'd just have to marry again.'

'Don't talk like that. Miles, what shall I do?'

There was no answer.

'Miles, what's the matter?'

'Nothing's the matter – just dropping off to sleep. What did you say?'

'Never mind – it wasn't important.'
'Tell me in the morning.'

Next day a note came for her from Steve. It said:

'Pushed on to Tibet sooner than I'd planned. This place is too crowded and I wouldn't like to put down any telltale roots. Meet you on the steps of the Shwe Dâgon on July 15th at 7 p.m. You will recognise me instantly by my green jungle battle-dress. Don't get strangled in the meantime. I doubt if he knows his own strength.

'Yours in haste, Steve.'

She did not show it to Miles. Although the Allies were still far away from Rangoon he might think Steve really meant it. She knew, of course, it was only a joke.

Chapter Ten

On the tenth day a telegram came for Miles. He was to report back to Delhi by the end of the week. He handed it over without speaking.

'Darling – it can't be true – how mean! Surely if you say it's your honeymoon you get compassionate leave?'

'They know it's my honeymoon. It must mean we're going forward.'

He looked as excited as a small boy before the holidays. She made one last attempt.

'Couldn't you ask the colonel if you could join them in Assam or wherever they are going?'

Miles took the telegram, folded it and placed it in his pocket.

'Can't do that sort of thing,' he sounded pompous. 'This is war, total war. We may be making an island landing.' He smiled smugly.

'Oh, no!'

'I'm only guessing, silly. I haven't an idea how the big boys plan to take Rangoon, but I do know this is no moment for personal considerations.'

'You don't love me or you wouldn't talk

169

like that.'

'Don't be childish, Lucy. Being married doesn't make it any easier to ignore Army orders. After all, you don't want me to get shot for desertion before I've even seen the Japanese?'

'Aren't you sorry at all?'

'Of course I'm sorry, darling, but we've had a wonderful ten days to be grateful for.'

'It should have been three weeks.' Her voice sounded unsteady.

'I know it should; it's very unfeeling of the authorities, but think of all the wives at home who haven't seen their husbands for two and three years?'

He put his hands on her shoulders. She leant against him crying hopelessly.

'It hasn't been long enough, I don't know you properly. I don't understand you. I can't guess what you think about. I love you. I shall die if you go away.'

'There, there,' Miles said, using his professional manner. 'Never mind, darling. I'll get leave again ever so soon, you'll see.'

'No, you won't – you'll be dead.'

'Lucy, do stop killing me off in my prime.'

'I shall kill myself too. I can't go on alone any more.'

'Enough melodrama. Now dry your eyes, and where shall we stay next time?'

'There aren't any hills in Burma.'

'We'll make a Tarzan hideout in the jungle,

or fly back to India.'

'It'll never be like this again, with our own home and this view and being away from everybody.'

'Nothing is ever the same – but it may be better.'

'You mean this hasn't been good enough for you?'

'That isn't what I said at all.'

'It's what you meant, though.'

'Don't get me wrong all the time.'

'I don't. I'm getting you right. You haven't been really happy or you wouldn't be so keen to go to Burma.'

She backed away from him against the sideboard, and he put his hand across his eyes.

'You expect too much, Lucy. You make it difficult for yourself.'

She looked out of the window and saw another day to begin the world with. She tried to be sensible.

'When must we go, Miles?'

'Tomorrow at latest – perhaps tonight.'

'Can we have one last good day – please?'

'That's up to you, darling.'

'I won't make a fuss – promise – if we can stay overnight.'

'What do you want to do?'

'Walk down to the Rilli – you know, that little river Steve was talking about.'

'Wouldn't it be more fun to go up higher?'

'But we could bathe in the Rilli.'

After five years of barbed-wire beaches or cold, muddy, weedy rivers at home, bathing in warmth and safety was luxury.

The first four miles sloped gently down the hill, the last two were a steep scramble.

An autumn feeling for English eyes – blue, blue distance and brown foreground, a tree with heavy, scarlet, rubbery flowers and no leaves; figs in fruit and bananas in flower, and a smell of orange blossom. Through bamboo groves, with water carried across the path in bamboo branches, they came to a man ploughing a strip, two feet wide and six feet long, and scattered tidy huts with neat flower gardens. Lower down the vegetation grew thicker and greener each side of the path and they saw big black butterflies like bats. At last, in the valley, spiky pineapple plantations and the lovely sound of running water.

They were both panting and her legs ached. They sat down on a rock and she slipped off her shoes and let the green water run over her feet.

'If the Japanese cut you off, Miles, and you have to trek across jungle country living on pineapples, you won't be in very good training.'

'This is the advance, darling, not the retreat. I shan't be cut off.'

172

'I can only hope so.'

She looked at him anxiously. He lay back on the hot rock still breathing heavily – he had pulled off his damp shirt.

'Oh, you are lovely.'

'Silly Lucy.'

'Why?'

'Men aren't lovely.'

'You are – even if you are scant of breath and all that muscle is really fat I'm mad about it.'

'Really, darling–'

'Well, why not? There is no one else in this whole valley, and if there were it would only be a fisherman who couldn't understand my compliments to you. Why shouldn't I admire my husband.'

Miles sat up and tweaked her nose.

'No reason at all. Shall we bathe or eat?'

'Bathe. Look – just a little further down there's a big pool, beyond that waterfall.'

Miles jumped in first while she was pulling her dress over her head. She lowered herself in more slowly:

'Do you think this comes off a glacier?'

The snow water licked her thighs. Miles swam across and holding her hands pulled her in on top of him, gasping. Snow took fire, enfolding water was feather soft. With pale, green, slippery summer limbs they floated gently together across to the other side, then Miles let her go and swam and splashed and dived and disappeared and came up smiling with the sleek head of an exhibitionist sea-lion. She soon climbed out and sat on a rock laughing at him.

'You're so strong, darling. I'm so impressed.'

He reached up and seized her ankle:

'I'll pull you in again if you mock me.'

'Not mocking – adoring.'

'Don't like the sound of it. I think I'll drown you.'

'Please not. I feel like a mermaid up here in the sun.'

'You'd feel even more like a mermaid down here in my dark pool.'

She twisted her ankle from his hand and started away across the rocks inland.

She heard a great splash as Miles heaved himself out of the water behind her, and she turned to laugh as he swore at a misplaced stone. He caught her as they reached the warm grass edge beyond the rocks.

PART III

Burma

Chapter Eleven

She saw Miles off from Delhi three days later. He was to report in Madras, presumably some attack on Japanese territory was being assembled there.

'Take care of yourself,' he said, through the carriage window. She could not speak, he looked so happy it was unbearable. He did not meet her anguished eyes.

'Sure to see you soon,' he added, patting the top of her head. 'I'll take Rangoon for you and then you can come in your canteen and give me a sausage roll.'

'Oh, Miles.'

'What's the matter?'

'Nothing. Just a twinge of despair – it'll pass.'

'Thought you must have got appendicitis.'

'Feels just about the same.'

Or more like that disease which dissolves all your bones to useless pulp, she thought.

'Shall I wait till the train goes?'

She wondered how much longer she would be strong enough to walk the platform.

'Don't bother – if you're in a hurry. I'm all right.'

I can see you are all right. I can see that

you do not in one corner of your splendid being need me at all.

'Perhaps I'll go, then.'

'Yes, do – better not keep Michèle waiting.'

'She won't mind – if you'd rather I stayed?'

'I tell you, Lucy, I'm all right. You go off and enjoy yourself.'

'Yes, Miles, of course, like hell.'

'Now, don't work yourself up, darling. It's going to be just the same as before I came.'

'Just the same – except that then I hadn't been married. Then I was just in love with you.'

'That's the girl–' Miles said vaguely. 'Now you run along and mind you write to me every week – and don't do anything you wouldn't do if I were there.'

'Such as?'

'Throwing all our wedding presents out of the window.'

The whistle blew.

'Oh, Miles – you're going – Miles, think about me sometimes – I only exist in you – keep me alive.'

She panted along beside the moving carriage hanging on to his hand. He tried to free himself.

'Be careful, darling. Let go – you'll fall down and sprain your ankle again.'

'Would you jump out if I did?'

'Of course not. You exaggerate so. Goodbye.'

He leant down and kissed her untidily, as he finally wrenched his hand away and was carried past the end of the platform.

She stood waving and sobbing long after the train was out of sight, until Michèle, tired of waiting in the station yard, touched her arm.

'He seems to have gone, Lucy.'

'How shall I manage?' she wailed.

'Cheer up – it won't be long. He's not the sort of man anything happens to – anything bad I mean.'

'But he's so brave – he'll dash into the front line. He's been longing for this.'

'My dear, they don't let the doctors get shot – they need them alive.'

'That's what Miles said, but he'd be the first to volunteer for dangerous reconnaissance.'

'They use Chindits for that – come on, Lucy. The world's still turning, and I've got some brandy in the taxi.'

'Drink won't help.'

'You'll be surprised. I've got through a lot of partings on brandy. Did you realise Sam and I will have to see you off in Calcutta when *you* go to the front? We'll need strong drinks for that too.'

'I wish you weren't leaving here next week.'

'All the better to greet you the other end.'

She suffered herself to be led out of the station and into the taxi. She sipped the brandy to please Michèle.

'Michèle, I don't know what I'd do without you.'

'Some lunatic thing like throwing yourself under the train to make Miles sit up and notice you, I expect.'

'I don't suppose he would have noticed – just have said "Bumpy, this line".'

'That's better.' Michèle filled up her glass. 'You must marry Sam.'

'He doesn't want to.'

'I don't get it.'

'Neither do I, but I've got no choice. Anyway, marriage seems to lead to a lot of tears.'

'But if I weren't married, I'd have to pretend I wasn't crying which is much more painful. At least I can admit now that I care.'

'Can you?'

'Well, I have anyway. Where are you going to stay in Calcutta?'

'Some good hotel.'

'Why Calcutta?'

'It's a big town they say. Plenty to do there. Sam's not restful, it's hard work keeping him amused.'

'Drink's not enough?'

'No. It has to be drink plus gaiety all day and night – and he gets up at 7 a.m. and says: *'Now* what shall we do?"'

'Poor Michèle. You of all people. No wonder the Americans get on so.'

'Don't let's think about it.' Michèle

poured some more brandy. They stepped out cautiously at the hostel, each carrying a full glass. Lucy paid the taxi and then followed Michèle, who also held the bottle, slowly upstairs to her room. She had not been back since the day before the wedding. She had spent the only night in Delhi with Miles at a hotel.

Smith was hovering in the passage.

'That doesn't look like lime juice,' he said ingratiatingly. 'How was the honeymoon?'

'Run away, Casanova,' Michèle slammed the door in his face and sat down on Lucy's bed.

'That's one man,' she said, 'that I really do not appreciate.'

'How shall I manage?' Lucy asked again, from her basket chair, but the urgency had gone. She saw now that her heart and lungs could probably carry on on their own for a while.

'How was it anyway?'

'What?'

'The honeymoon.'

'Not long enough.'

I don't know the beginning of him and this may be the end. She began to cry again but her sorrow was softer.

'Hey,' Michèle handed her another handkerchief. 'Don't start all over again, I shouldn't have mentioned it. Let's pass on to the weather. Cooking up down here. Did

181

you notice a difference?'

'Yes.'

'Some people like dry heat it seems, and some damp. Delhi is dry, stoke-oven type. Calcutta is Turkish bath. Which do you prefer?'

'Neither – they both make me feel frantic, as if the top of my head was coming off. Is it?'

'No, but I see the blonde is growing out. Are you going to Madame again?'

'No, I think black will be more seemly for a grass widowhood. I shan't see anybody till Miles comes on leave. I shall live very quietly.'

'Oh, yes.'

'Well, why should I go out?'

'No reason at all. But I'd like to know how you are going to avoid it.'

'By saying no.'

So she said 'no' to everyone for three weeks, except McCleod who offered to see her off on the night train to Calcutta. The Ministry stopped a month's pay because she had not stayed her scheduled three years. She had refused to take any money from Miles before he left, saying she had plenty, and now did not like to bother him with her long row with the authorities. She reckoned she had enough to get to Assam and there the Women's Canteen Force (Burma) would

182

look after her or perhaps Miles really would be in Burma too. She had not heard for a week, which meant he was probably on the move. She paid off the hostel and McCleod drove down to the station with her.

'Let's hope this journey is more successful than the last time I took you in a taxi.'

'It can't break down – I can't afford a hitch.'

'Shall I lend you some money, Lucy?'

'No, thanks. I'm fine as long as things go all right.'

She was feeling extraordinary. McCleod's black beard swayed about in front of her. Sometimes quite close, sometimes far away. The back of the driver's turbaned head looked like a hard-boiled egg. Her throat was raw.

'Would you say I had a fever?'

McCleod felt her forehead.

'Definitely,' he said, whipping a thermometer out of his pocket.

'Do you always carry one?'

'Yes, I get malaria, and it amuses me to see where I can push it up to.'

'Hundred and three degrees,' McCleod announced as the taxi stopped at the station and a porter fell on her luggage.

'Oh damn.'

'We'd better go back to New Delhi.'

'No – I can't. I've said good-bye to everyone and given up my room and I can't afford a hotel.'

'I'll lend you money. I said so.'

'No – really – it's too much anticlimax. You know what fevers are in this country – here today, gone tomorrow.'

'Or dead,' McCleod said cheerfully.

Gerard, the other Englishman in the newsroom, had died in three days in Calcutta of cholera without going anywhere near the Japanese. Perhaps Miles was even now being torpedoed in the Burmese Ocean.

'I'm going on,' she said, firmly through chattering teeth. 'If I break down in Calcutta Michèle is there, and once I reach Assam there are hordes of good ladies who will nurse me.'

'I think I ought to stop you for Miles's sake.'

'He wouldn't worry – doctors never fuss about other people's illnesses.'

It was a four-berth sleeping compartment. The other three occupants were men and looked at her sourly, one going so far as to mutter that he thought things had been very badly arranged. She turned her face to the wall below and with four aspirins inside her began the dizzy descent to normal as the train rattled out across the plain.

She saw with intense homesickness Rachel and Henry laughing in an English pub, going home to English pork pie, pulling on plenty of blankets at night for a chilly English May. It seemed unbelievable that she and Miles would ever be together under an English roof. She did not even know what sort of roof he liked, flats or houses? Furniture from Heal's or from Maple's? Or run up by a little man? They had never discussed the future. Why had he never mentioned children? Did he like gardening? Would it be a country practice? Or surgery in town?

The train made strange clicks and clankings in the deepest night and she imagined the oiled bodies of Indian robbers and murderers pushing up the shutters silently, slithering in, taking everything, if necessary life, without a squeak from their victims. She slept at last, hurtling into a nightmare world where Miles was a naked bandit slitting her appendix with expert precision.

'This will hardly hurt,' he said jovially, raising a gleaming bread-knife.

She woke, choking with fright, to a hot and gritty dawn. All day clothes stuck to dripping limbs and each object touched with clammy hands was rough with dust. The three officers tried to teach her to play bridge, but, baffled by her stupidity, they ended in whist. With evening she could feel the fever rising again and fell into a second night of nightmares more furious than the first.

She arrived at Calcutta in the morning

feeling as if her legs would fold under her, but knew her temperature was down. She took a taxi to Michèle's hotel and found them breakfasting in bed. Sam sent for another tray and Lucy drank about two pints of tea and felt better.

'You look awful,' Michèle said, spooning a slice of pawpaw.

'Nothing to what I feel. I think I must have got sand-fly fever.'

'What's that?' Sam asked. 'Is it catching?' He sat up looking anxious.

'No – just uncomfortable.'

He lay down again and picked up the *Statesman*.

'We're going swimming,' Michèle told her. 'What about you?'

'My train's at lunch-time. I'd like to sleep till then.'

'We'll take you across.'

She got up and went to run a bath.

'How's Miles?' Sam asked through the newspaper.

'Well, as far as I know.'

'Fine – fine,' Sam said. 'Can you get that woman of mine to step on it? I've never known a female take so long to dress.'

She went through to the bathroom and made a slight effort to hurry Michèle, who only turned on more hot water with her toe.

'Let him wait,' she said. 'He's always like that. Eating his head off to go places. What for? Each place in this godawful town is awfuller than the last. Heard from Miles?'

'Not for ten days – I expect he's on the move. He doesn't like writing letters anyway.'

'Neither do I – hope you aren't hoping I'll write to you at the front.'

'Of course not – I don't hope anything. Have you any aspirins? I've run out.'

'On the glass shelf. Hadn't you better stay here a few days, Lucy? You don't look fit to go out to tea, let alone join the Army.'

'Can't afford to.'

'Sam'd pay – he's got far more money than is good for him.'

'No, thanks, I want to get on now I've started. I'm better now.'

'Like hell you are. I never saw anyone look so better.'

Sam banged on the door.

'Stop flattering in there. I'm all set,' he roared.

Michèle got out languidly and putting one foot up on the bath began to paint her toe-nails. Lucy went back into the bedroom.

'Not more than another half-hour,' she told Sam. She lay back on the empty bed and closed her eyes. Sam drew the sheet over her.

'I'm not quite a corpse yet.'

'I know – I'm leaving you breathing space.'

She was asleep in three minutes. She slept

through their departure for the swimming-bath, and would have slept through the time of the train if they had not returned for her at noon. She refused the drinks they offered and drove to the station with a very blurred impression of Calcutta sweltering in early summer. They waited while she went off to report as instructed to the R.T.O's office.

'Private Spender,' she told him. 'Going to join up, W.C.F.'

He had no record of her existence.

'But I booked a berth. I thought they fixed this train for me?'

Nothing – no reservation, no record, no room on the train.

'Come back in three days,' he said. 'Probably fix you up then.'

'But where can I go?'

'The Y.W.C.A. is very good.'

'But I've no money.'

At this point she burst into tears, enraged with herself but too feeble to stop. It was some minutes before she realised that the R.T.O. had become human and was patting her on the back.

'Look,' he said. 'Don't take on, lass. I'll see what I can do. Would you mind sitting up all night?'

'Anything to get out of here. Of course I don't mind.'

'Then I'll pop you into the odd chair in a ladies' compartment. How's that?'

188

'Heaven.'

'Come on, then.'

She shambled after him up the train. Michèle took her arm when she saw her face.

'Lucy, you are the most tearful woman I ever met. Now what's thwarting you?'

'They said there wasn't a place on the train.'

'I'll fix that,' Sam said bringing out a roll of rupee notes.

'No, don't, Sam – it's all right. Tears are cheaper. It's fixed.'

Luckily the R.T.O. was well ahead and did not hear.

She wondered if she would ever see Michèle again. After the war did not mean Kentucky for her, or Victoria station. Perhaps, driving with Miles across Paris to the Gare du Nord they would catch a glimpse of her – neat, small, silent, provocative as a cat – tripping down the Boulevard des Capucines. Michèle wrinkled her nose now to steady her dark glasses.

'Bash them,' she urged, as Lucy looked down at her on the platform.

'Who?'

'The Japs, the British, the char and wads, anything within reach.' She cackled.

'Why don't you go with Lucy?' Sam asked her. 'Just the life for a girl.'

'Too much like hard work,' Michèle slipped her arm into his. They waved twice as the train drew out and then Lucy saw them turn away. Sam must be hustling her off to more places for more drinks.

Chapter Twelve

The train came into Assam from Bengal before dark, a much greener country. The rain streamed down and at every station white-clothed Indians gathered under black umbrellas. Vultures with straight, out-stretched wings were standing in the fields. It was cooler and the fever did not return. In the morning they crossed the Brahmaputra in a ferry. It had rained all night, the sky was still cloudy and the wide river dull and sulky.

An Air Force lorry took her up to an Army depot where she sat about for two hours, getting hotter and stickier every minute, waiting for the next stage in the journey. This time she joined a convoy for the hills. They drove past pink flowering tamarisk, then through a stretch of real jungle in-habited by fearless tigers and panthers who had been known to jump on to the bonnets of jeeps at night. After the jungle came open country, very bright green hills with paddy in the valleys, hills like the lowlands of Scot-land with scattered rocks. Then the pines began, herds of chestnut horses galloped through the brown woods in the sun, beyond them the white tents of a Remount Camp and a silver river. The last ten miles twisted steeply uphill through pine woods. The smell was intoxicating, and when she heard the first cuckoo she was as enchanted as any veteran letter-writer to *The Times*.

Her training centre was in a town of red corrugated iron scattered along the top of a hill. The lorry dropped her at another transport officer's depot and he telephoned to the W.C.F. while she sat peacefully on her luggage beside the road.

The senior officer who came to fetch her was a charming, plump, middle-aged lady who drove the jeep with alarming rapidity until it broke down in a peach orchard.

'Oh dear,' she said. 'What shall we do?'

Lucy found this behaviour very reassuring. She had been nervously dreading the ferocious efficiency of female Army officers. A small stream ran across the orchard, behind stood two barns, one white and one wooden, with thatched roofs.

'I like it here,' she said unhelpfully.

'Yes, dear, but it's pleasant up at the house, too, and nearly tea-time. Don't you know anything about jeeps?'

'I'm afraid not.'

'Neither do I,' said Mrs Watney-Cox cheerfully, 'so it's no good my getting out and peering into the bonnet. Someone will be along soon. Have a barley sugar – glucose, and most sustaining. Where's your husband?'

Lucy told her. She talked about Miles for nearly five minutes. Mrs Watney-Cox smiled kindly without looking at all bored, though she suddenly interrupted her to shriek as she saw another jeep coming up the road.

'Oh, Captain Morrison, what shall we do? The jeep's gone wrong again.'

'Have to get you a new one.'

Captain Morrison and his whiskers reined in alongside.

'Yes, it's the second time this week. I don't know what I do to it.'

'Out of petrol?'

'Oh, do you think it could be that?'

'Easily – anyway you put her in neutral and I'll push you up the hill.'

He backed off and came at them again from behind.

'Splendid,' Mrs Watney-Cox beamed, as they were propelled up and through the drive gates and free-wheeled down to the house. 'Come to tea,' she shouted back, but Captain Morrison was already out of earshot.

'Dear boys,' she added vaguely. 'They're all so good to us.'

She led Lucy into the house to meet the sixteen girls who were living in Cleethorpes at the time, English girls from Kenya, and all over India, none of whom had been in

England since before the war. Up here in Assam they trained and assembled their uniforms before going off to the forward areas. She would be kept here for at least a month.

It poured with rain before a flashing sun, and the cuckoo deep in the pine woods never stopped. Lucy was sent to sleep in a near-by bungalow. A damp little Ghurka guarded the door. Her first night she was very miserable. She felt cold and ill in bed, and woke to feel in the dark insects moving all over her. She jumped out and lit a candle and found the sheets crawling with bed bugs. She killed over a dozen before she could sleep and then a blinding thunderstorm gave her nightmares about the end of the world.

Work on the Canteen began next morning. She was not very good at it. She never could count in shillings and pence – without adding rupees, annas and, at some units, Hindustani to it. For several nights she fell asleep hearing those urgent Indian voices trying to buy soap from her: *'Kangha hal? Tarch hal? Sarbon mangta, polls, bros, mithai mangta.'*

The fourth day a short letter came from Miles with a field post office address, so at least he was not yet at sea – or had not been a week ago. Mrs. Watney-Cox sent her out to 'do the flowers' like any lady, and she picked an armful of pinks, sweet williams, tiger lilies, snapdragons and cherry pie from the garden. In the sunshine she heard goat-bells in the distance as well as the cuckoo.

Every evening they were expected to go out. Invitations showered in from units stationed in the area to dances, whist drives and parties. To celebrate the end of the European war they were fetched by two airmen called Jock and Sandy in a truck to attend a barbecue in the open air.

It was exactly like Hell. People packed tight together on a small canvas dance floor jigged frantically up and down outlined black against a great bonfire, with a back-drop of showering fireworks. There was a pervading smell of roasting flesh and gun-powder. A row of pathetic senior officers sat trapped in deck-chairs behind the ropes. One of them handed Lucy, without a word, a charred piece of ox. There were drunks about everywhere and Sandy had to clear one from under the wheels of the truck before he could move it when he suggested a trip up to the hospital for refreshments. Jock, it seemed, was really on night duty there. They found most of the patients up, wandering about restlessly, drinking their beer ration. They ate sandwiches in the ward kitchen while Jock told them how he had been all round the world before his father's legacy ran out, and the best way to handle an epileptic. They left him behind and drove back to the battlefield about ten o'clock only to find that the authorities had closed down the whole show.

She had been a private for over a fortnight when the telegram came from Steve. It read:

(a) Are you there?
(b) Is Major Spender there?

She replied: (a) Yes (b) No (c) Why? to a Calcutta address he gave her.

Two days later she was detailed to fetch firewood for the house from a lumber depot just on the edge of the woods outside the town. This was a pleasant job. She spent a happy afternoon sitting on top of a high pile of pine logs, while a warm sun chased around in small clouds, watching the poor minions staggering about and heaving tree-trunks up into the truck. The truck was nearly full when a jeep bounded across the field and swerved to a stop below her. Steve jumped out shouting:

'What a girl – what a girl!' and rushed the barricades.

'Look out,' she yelled, as the logs began to slip, but it was too late. The whole pile rumbled down and threw both of them on to the grass.

They sat up laughing.

'You look marvellous – it suits you – hurrah for the girls in jungle green.'

Steve was still shouting. He kissed her several times between shouts.

'I'm just here,' she yelled. 'I can hear you quite well. What are *you* doing here?' She tried to stand up out of range of Steve's arms – she was covered with sawdust and weak with laughter.

'Enjoying myself,' Steve said, kissing her again.

'Stop it, then – you are giving the servants the wrong impression.'

'Impossible – they reckon all the *sahibs* are mad, they aren't even looking. Are you a widow yet?'

'Of course not.'

'Pity.'

'Have a heart.'

'That's my trouble.'

She succeeded in getting to her feet and tried to be serious:

'Look, Steve–'

'Wonderful – she's remembered my name.'

'And mine–?'

'Brenda, would it be, or Bridget? Or Madeleine the best of all?'

'What had Madeleine got?'

'She hadn't a husband for a start.'

'But you obviously find my husband an added attraction. You paid no attention to me single.'

'Maybe, provided he isn't here. You are sure he isn't being a nigger just behind that woodpile?'

'Quite sure, unfortunately; he's on his way to Burma.'

'So am I.'

'Looks like it. Steve, listen—'

'Not a word will be wasted. I love to hear your silky, soft voice. I could listen to it all night. Come to think of it, best by night, by candlelight, with a dip of a winged whisper in it—'

'I am in the middle of fetching the wood,' she bellowed. 'I have to go away in that truck now, sitting by that Sikh driver. When I get the other end I have to sit down for another half-hour while the little men store it in the wood-shed.'

'Hurrah for the wood-shed!' Steve made a swoop at her and carried her kicking over to his jeep.

'No more corny jokes,' she implored him.

'Not just the one?'

'Particularly not that one.'

He let in the clutch and they shot level with the Sikh driver. She sobered up enough to order the driver home, then Steve was off, leaping the jeep away ahead of the truck.

'How did you know I was out here?' she asked.

'Enquired at H.Q. for Private Spender.

Heard you were on wood fatigue – a darling of a girl told me the way.'

'Which girl?' she asked, too quickly, and he turned on her laughing again:

'Major Watney-Cox – nicest girl I've met for years. Seemed all in favour of me.'

'She probably thought you were Miles. She's very kind-hearted and romantic.'

'Shall we pretend I am?'

'No. Don't be ridiculous.'

'What's so ridiculous about that?'

'Everything – oh, you do drive deliciously fast.'

She stood up and leant on the windscreen and let the wind into her hair. She thought Steve would tell her to sit down but he only swung round the bends faster than ever, singing at the top of his voice.

She took him into Cleethorpes and left him alone in an arm-chair by a bunch of sweet peas, while she went out to see the wood stowed away. She was humming from head to foot, and could not sit still while the men meandered about, but demeaned her *mem-sahib* status by throwing logs into the shed with her own bare hands. By the time she had washed and changed and got the tangles out of her hair she came back to find Steve eating buttered toast surrounded by eager girls.

'I'm quite all right,' he told her with his mouth full. 'Being very well looked after.'

Mary handed him a pink-iced cake. Margaret filled his tea-cup and Isabel said: 'Do go on. What did the chief of the Maquis do then?' with her blue eyes round and believing. Lucy helped herself and sat down quietly near the fire to hear Steve's fairy-story.

The next day was Sunday. Steve was at the front door by ten o'clock.

'Come on,' he said, 'out for the day.'

'Oh, no.' She appealed to Mrs Watney-Cox. 'I'm not allowed to – am I?'

She only smiled indulgently.

'All right, Lucy, off you go – we can manage without you.'

'What about the stores?'

'Isabel can do them.'

She stepped into the jeep, resigned to enjoyment.

'Where are we going?' she asked Steve as they left the pine woods behind and came out higher up to low hills and rocks.

'Cherrapunji – the wettest place on earth.'

'Whatever for?'

'It really is the wettest place on earth. I want to see it.'

They had started in sunshine, but halfway there a thick white mist came down and they drove the rest of the way in a cloud. Sometimes the cloud drifted apart to show a sunlit valley miles below. They reached

Cherrapunji at noon, a village of little stone white-washed houses with tin roofs, standing in undulating green country in driving rain. The Welsh mission seemed to have influenced the landscape and the weather, as well as the architecture.

'One myth exploded,' Steve said. 'They told me it never rains when you come here.'

'Oh, really?'

She shook the water out of her hair as they went into the Dak bungalow. Steve lit a fire and they sat in front of it over a meal of fried eggs and tinned peaches and cake and tea which Steve produced from a knapsack.

'What a wonderful cook you are, dear Lucy.'

'I did a course at the Cordon Bleu.'

'Good education is never wasted – but I'm sorry I forgot the milk.'

'Sugar is much more comforting.'

'Sitting there with your bare toes to the flames you almost make me believe in hearth and home.'

She tried to look less happy.

'Perhaps I'd better warn you,' he went on, 'before you relax too thoroughly, that we are going to look at some caves as soon as you've drunk your tea.'

'Oh, no – it's still raining.'

'No, it's stopped. The sound you hear is only the roof dripping.'

She got back reluctantly into the damp

jeep and they drove on to another village. Steve asked a group of children the way and they pointed straight across a river. Without a moment's hesitation, Steve drove the jeep into the middle of the torrent.

'It must be far too deep,' she screamed, preparing to jump for her life. But the river was quite shallow, the water only came in over their feet; when they reached the opposite bank she looked upstream and saw a perfectly good bridge about thirty yards away, which had been hidden by a bend, over this bridge came the village children again shouting and laughing.

'Oh, Steve.'

'Never mind, we've made a local legend.'

He stopped and waited for the children to catch up. They climbed on the bonnet and hung on to the doors: nothing so exciting had happened that way for years.

After a time Steve got out and shook them all off and picked the three tallest volunteers as guides to the caves. It was an exhausting walk, during which they waded across four streams and pushed through nasty-looking jungle before the three boys stopped proudly in front of an overgrown hole which they claimed to be the entrance to the caves.

Steve started to laugh.

'After all that – obviously they hadn't an idea what I was after.'

'Perhaps this really is the cave.'

She stooped down and peered into the small darkness. It looked an ideal home for a cobra.

'No – they were real good caves. I've heard them described by people who'd been there. Never mind.'

They turned round and trudged back through the jungle and the four streams to the jeep. She came out of the last stream with leeches on her legs.

'Help – help!' she screamed, losing all control at once. 'I'll be sucked dry. I'm dying.'

She hopped about on the bank to the astonishment of the little boys and the delight of Steve, who was laughing so much that it was several minutes before he could get a good glow on his cigarette to burn off the bloodsuckers. She sat down weakly in the jeep.

'Do you think I should have a blood transfusion?'

Steve hugged her as he took the brake off and began to bump the jeep towards the bridge.

'Darling, I adore you.'

'But you aren't taking me seriously. Suppose I've lost gallons of blood?'

'Your eyes have swollen to saucers.'

'Probably a symptom of acute blood deficiency.'

'I think you'll pull through – after another cup of strong, sweet tea.'

'Thank goodness. Are we going to make tea now?'

'Not just yet. We have to see the famous view first.'

She tried to resist the view when he drew up alongside a rock which he assured her was known as the suicide rock.

'I shall only get dizzy.'

But he dragged her out firmly.

'You'll never be here again. Keep your eyes open now.'

'Faint from loss of blood,' she murmured, but he supported her faltering steps and led her to the edge of the precipice.

Four thousand feet below the plains were blue, parrot-green, and silver with flooded paddy-fields; they stood far above flocks of scattered white woolly clouds.

'It was worth the walk,' Steve remarked. She could not think of anything to say; there is nothing to be said about a breath-taking view except 'Oh, look,' and Steve was doing that already.

'What a pity,' Steve added, 'it is so far from anywhere where one might feel like committing suicide.'

'People must have felt like it here or they wouldn't have that jolly name for it.'

'I don't believe they lived here. They travelled across continents for the pleasure of taking off so many thousand feet at one jump.'

'If it often rains like today even the inhabitants may get desperate.'

'It's starting again. Hurry.'

She forgot her leech-wounded legs and ran as fast as Steve to the slight shelter of the jeep.

Back in the Dak bungalow they finished up the cake and the tea and dried out their shoes. They started the homeward journey in sunshine, but by half past five it was raining so hard that Steve drew in to the side of the road and stopped the engine.

'Can't see a damn thing,' he said cheerfully.

The rain came down in solid sheets, like a film about a hurricane. It dashed on the ground with snowy whiteness. Steve tried to light a cigarette, but it was hopeless, everything they possessed was sodden. Her hair stuck to her ears.

'What a bloody awful day to offer a loved one.'

But he blew the rain off the end of his nose and laughed.

'Or even just a friend,' she said, as she steamed with happiness inside her mackintosh cape. She could not imagine ever looking less attractive, or more thoroughly damp.

'I shan't forget today.'

'The wettest day of your life? That invisible sun within you should dry your clothes in no time.'

'Did you get to Lhasa?'

'Of course not – driven out with ignominy just past the frontier.'

'Steve, don't you think we'd better drive on?'

'I can't see either side of the road yet, so I might take you over one of the precipices, but if you insist– '

'Oh, no – not if it's like that. But what are we going to do?'

'Or make love?'

'Or go fishing makes more sense right now.'

'But some other time?'

'Of course not. I'm in love with Miles – not just married to him.'

'Naturally, my darling, but you hadn't reckoned on me.'

'Why shouldn't I have reckoned on you? Nobody could possibly look at you once they'd seen Miles.'

'Try looking at me now to pass the time.'

She kept on rubbing her wet hands with a damp handkerchief till he tilted her face up and she had to look. His curly hair lay flat with rains His whole face was wet, but his eyes were burning.

'Oh damn,' she said. 'Why me?'

'And why me?' he answered, quietly.

'But it isn't possibly you – I've got Miles, don't you understand? I don't *want* anybody else.'

'It isn't what you want, it's what you get.'

He suddenly laughed again, and started the jeep, nosing forward into a clear evening of strong, gold light, with purple streaks on the green hills and a rainbow bridging a narrow valley.

Chapter Thirteen

She left the hills of Assam in the dawn by bus a few weeks later, with four other girls and three Indian cooks. It was cold and fortunately too misty to see the precipices on the long twisting descent, the driver kept turning round to count his passengers or talk to his friends.

In the plain, purple jacarandas along the road dripped in steady rain. They waited several hours at the railway station, eating pineapples, drinking tea and playing whist. When the train at last arrived they jumbled into one carriage with twenty-three pieces of luggage. Two hours later they had to change, in the dark, without porters, the cooks had disappeared. Isabel, the corporal in charge, wrung her hands hysterically, but they piled her with baggage till she had no hands free to wring, and all staggered up one long platform and down another to the next train where they fell gasping and giggling into their reserved carriage, only to find that it had no light.

'Are you all here?' Isabel asked anxiously. 'Margaret, Joan, Lucy – help, where's Mary?'

Mary's voice came muffled from under a bedding roll.

'What shall I do? I can't possibly count the luggage if I can't see it.'

Isabel sounded nearly in tears. They all felt around, under and beside them. The total they now arrived at was twenty-nine.

'What about the hurricane lamps?' Joan suggested. 'Any matches?'

As the train jerked into life the lamp was lit and the luggage loomed up all round their flushed faces.

'What a way to go to war,' someone said.

One of the cooks appeared, whimpering at the window in the middle of the night to say a major had turned him out of his carriage. For one stupid, sleepy moment, Lucy wondered if she could possibly be on the same train as Miles. An officer removed the cook and stowed him in somewhere else.

Round the breakfast table in Chittagong they saw for the first time the yellow, jaundiced faces of those who had regularly taken their anti-malaria tablets.

During the next five days of uncertainty and inactivity Lucy met several members of the canteen force who had come back to rest, or go on leave, from the forward areas. She realised with increasing nervousness that she was in the wrong *galère;* they told hair-raising tales of bravery and danger on the road to Mandalay in very close proximity to the Japanese. Her admiration for them increased daily, so did her apprehension, but they assured her that the bad part of the campaign was over, it was too late to have any opportunity of roughing it even, let alone coming into contact with the enemy.

They were sent to the airstrip early on a Sunday morning, and sat for four hours on the ground under a brassy sky, waiting for a plane. For the first hour they found some shade behind a stationary truck, and played cards. But when the truck drove away, the game stopped.

At noon they were stuffed into two American transport planes. Mary and Lucy and crates of tinned fruit, and sausage-meat, and tea and tooth-brushes were loaded into the first plane, four other girls and three cooks disappeared into the second.

The American crew treated them very kindly, though Lucy felt they were carrying hospitality too far when they pressed Mary to take the controls over enemy-occupied territory. Mary, a lively and enterprising girl, accepted at once. The pilot's door was then closed, and in the body of the plane Lucy tried hard to keep her mind on the game of poker she was playing with the engineer, but found the view of clouds, green islands, distant shining sea, and luscious feathery jungle no longer attractive.

In Rangoon they waited another hour on

the airstrip, sitting on the crates and boxes to keep their feet dry. Lucy was driven to a unit billeted near the airstrip.

The house was at first sight delightful. It had two storeys and stood in a garden, the last in a road, with open country behind. The Japanese (or the Allies) had blown all the glass out of the windows and pitted the walls with gunfire, but everywhere downstairs the red-tiled floor was scrubbed and shining and the living-room had yellow cotton curtains and cushion covers.

In the dining-room a bowl of red flowers stood on a green-and-white check cloth, and as Lucy walked in, someone put a record of 'Bist du bei mir' on a gramophone.

There were five women in the unit. Eleanor, the captain, who slept alone in a small room over the porch, Greta, the sergeant, who also slept alone because she was older than the others, and in the third room the other ranks, Jennifer, Elizabeth and Lucy.

Greta's husband had been years in the Burmese Civil. They had walked out of Burma together in the retreat, followed by a stout white spaniel, Nelly. They were now all back again, including Nelly, who had ridden in with Greta via Mandalay. Greta said Nelly was pleased to be home, but the poor dog only lay all day on the veranda panting sadly in the monsoon heat.

Jennifer and Elizabeth were seventeen and eighteen, one well-rounded and mouse-coloured, one slim and fair. Jennifer had been longest in the Army and seemed likely to get one stripe first.

Lucy sat down with pleasure to Burmese curry and tinned peaches at lunch-time, but soon lost her appetite as Greta described what had happened to her only the day before.

The internal plumbing of the house had been wrecked so there was a wooden latrine in a tent in the garden. Greta had been sitting there quietly, when she suddenly got the funny feeling that she was not alone in the tent – there was somebody breathing behind her. She looked round to see a full-grown python, as wide as a man's thigh, heaving its way in. About half of it had already negotiated the tent flap. Greta did not wait for the back half, but shot forward out into the sunlight, shrieking, with her trousers round her ankles.

'It's quite all right now,' she finished, to encourage Lucy. 'The Indians have cut back the jungle behind and frightened it away.'

It was many nights, however, before Lucy was brave enough to venture out after dark to the tent with no weapon against pythons but a flickering hurricane lamp; and after a sloughed snake-skin was found one morn-

212

ing under Jennifer's bed, she never got into her own bed without stripping back the sheet and looking under the pillow and on top of the mosquito-net.

She thought Greta might help her to get news of Miles. Greta's husband already worked in an office in Rangoon, though still disguised as a colonel.

'Don't worry, child,' Greta said. 'He'll find you in an hour once he reaches Rangoon. There aren't so many of us here, he only has to ask at our headquarters.'

'Perhaps he's already been through and gone up-country to the fighting,' Lucy suggested gloomily.

'Surely he'd have left a message here then?'

It sounded sensible. She threw herself into the job and tried to obliterate anxiety.

They worked a canteen on the airstrip in three shifts, one at a time for three hours. The rest of the day they checked stores, did accounts, and took a mobile canteen round to units in outlying villages. By the end of the working day one was ready to relax with one's feet up, but there was seldom any rest before midnight. Units for miles around, and as far away as Rangoon itself, sent trucks or jeeps to pick them up for parties and dances. There were several thousand men stationed round the airstrip for a start, many thousands more in the whole area who considered it the duty of at least one of the five women, though preferably all, to grace their social functions.

'Marvellous time you girls have,' they told Lucy, pushing her hotly round the dance floor.

Often her eyes shut from exhaustion and she stumbled through the steps half asleep. They drove out in full monsoon downpours, arriving at their destinations with long dresses wet and muddy to the knees. After a few dances the dresses would also be soaking from neck to waist and clinging to one's prickly heat.

'Let's sit this one out,' Lucy implored.

'Not *my* dance – I haven't had a dance all evening. Sit the next one out with Taffy.'

But with Taffy it was the same story.

'You can't sit *this* one out – it's a tango. I'm a demon for the tango.'

And he was, too – fling you to right, seize you to left, round you go, back you go, out for the promenade.

'Please, Taffy, I can't keep on, honestly.'

''Course you can, doing fine, that's the girl, just follow me.'

She discovered that up to and including the rank of sergeant, the Army and the Air Force were keen and efficient dancers with years of practice behind them. Warrant officers were a toss up, and once you reached lieutenants and pilot officers they were almost certain to be no good. Which did not prevent them, in their arrogance, keeping you moving to the music for just as long.

One day after a particularly infuriating evening dancing on a hard tennis court in an officers' mess, she sent off an enraged letter to a Forces paper which circulated all over Asia, saying that in her opinion the other ranks suffered from a ridiculous inferiority complex, and were much better dancers than either officers or Americans. She signed herself 'Pte. Lucy Spender (W.C.F.)'.

It rained and rained and rained. Green mould grew on the shoes overnight. Jennifer suffered most from prickly heat. She stood on the bedroom balcony naked in the rain and then sat dripping to struggle with the canteen accounts.

'Highly operational,' she murmured when Lucy commented on this method of doing arithmetic. Her pilot boy friend had given her a black kitten. Lucy had a new wrench of longing for Miles when Jennifer carried it triumphantly into their bedroom one evening. Jim, the pilot, had told her it would die.

'I've brought up bears, hyenas, crocodiles and skunks,' she told them indignantly. 'I don't need anyone to tell me how to bring up an ordinary cat.'

'I had a cat in India and it was murdered,' Lucy said.

'Careless girl.'

'I couldn't have helped it – another cat did it.'

'Well, there isn't another cat for miles around here.'

'You watch out the python doesn't get it.'

Jennifer, brought up to expect pythons at the bottom of the garden, was not afraid.

A few days later Lucy met her staggering into the house, tears in her eyes, with a big white paddy bird in her arms.

'Those boys,' she said, 'they think it's madly gay to shoot things and they can't even do it properly.'

She laid the dying paddy bird out on a cushion on the floor of the bedroom and wept over it while the kitten tweaked its tail feathers.

Miles wrote at last to say he had moved farther south in India. Lucy read the letter four times, but it was bleak.

'There is nothing to tell you about my work here, all routine stuff.'

She longed to hear everything he did every day. He had been to a dance and met some pretty nurses, 'but they had nothing to say for themselves,' he added, and she could not be sure whether to be jealous or not. He still hoped to be in Burma soon, and hoped she was all right. He ended 'love from Miles'. He did not say he missed her.

It was late afternoon and the canteen

empty, except for two airmen quietly playing darts in one corner; beside them lay their bush hats, stuffed with the cakes they were taking back to the rest of the squadron. Mogul and Chitti, the two Burmese boys who watched the fire, were asleep on the floor of the kitchen. Through the open doorway she watched a Dakota come in along the airstrip.

She pulled out Miles's photograph and studied it behind the tea urn, to reassure herself that he did exist and was her husband, until a corporal, dressed, like most of the customers, only in a pair of old shorts, leaned across the sausage rolls to ask who was the glamour boy, as he held out his tin mug. She pushed Miles back into her pocket, blushing, and apologising.

She thought the corporal would go away when he had his tea, but he leant up against the counter to chat.

'Boy friend in Burma?' he asked.

'My husband – no, not yet – he's still in India.'

'Coming this way?'

'I think he may be going further, for a landing against the Japanese.'

'Poor sod,' said the corporal brightly.

'They manage landings very efficiently now,' she pointed out to reassure herself. She came round in front of the counter and began to fold the blue-and-white check

217

tablecloths for the end of another day.

'Yes, better than they did. I was at Dunkirk.'

'You couldn't call that a landing exactly.'

'No – an amphibious operation, though. I was in the old *Lancastria,* sank June 16th, 1940, six miles off St. Nazaire.'

'I don't believe they lose so many ships this end of the war.'

She did not want to hear. She rattled the gramophone records back into their box.

'They'd better not – it was murder.' The corporal's eyes shone. 'I jumped eighty foot into the sea wearing full battle-dress, tin hat, the works... Couldn't swim, so much stuff on, the lifebelt didn't hold me up – threw away the titfer and was still floating up to my nose. Chap came past me then doing the crawl as cool as if he was in the Serpentine. "Push down on it, mate," he told me. Three thousand died. Saw five hundred on the upturned end of the boat singing "Roll out the Barrel", community singing like a Cup Final and no chance of rescue. I'm not at all brave, if anything I'm inclined to be a bit windy, but funny thing, I never thought anything could happen to *me*.'

He smiled at her cheerfully.

Miles never thought things could happen to him either, so perhaps he would manage to keep his nose clear above the sea.

Chapter Fourteen

The end of the week, her letter to the newspaper was published, an airman brought it into the canteen.

'I see you've been slumming,' he remarked. 'Fancy a respectable girl like you going dancing with the other ranks.'

She defended herself hotly, but he blandly refused to believe she could possibly be serious.

She was teased all day by incredulous other ranks at the canteen and was already tired of the whole subject when she got back to the house to find a senior officer (female) waiting for her with a strong reprimand. It seemed that it was illegal, or at any rate not done, for a lady in the W.C.F. to have her name in print. She had disgraced the whole force by her flippancy and probably ruined her chances of promotion.

She crawled to bed in a stupor of misery, beginning to wonder what she had done, but it wasn't till the following week when the letters started to roll in from all over South-East Asia that the enormity of her crime was brought home to her.

Letters arrived from units, from submarines, from lonely outposts, in batches, singly, sometimes twenty a day. When the flood was ended, she counted over seven hundred. Only a very few of the hundreds were friendly, those of course were too friendly, offering marriage, or a good time on leave with plenty of dancing, but the majority were sadly vituperative. Some, more sorry than angry, merely said she had not been out long enough to realise the situation, others were frankly furious, blaming the English girl for all the loneliness and misery of the British soldier.

On her head were heaped the sins of every wife and sweetheart who had gone off with Poles, with Americans, with Czechoslovakians, forgetting, along with the rest of England, the slogging, sweating, unspectacular Fourteenth Army. They detailed endless dreary stories of the snobbery of white women in the Far East.

The girl who said to the corporal 'I'm sorry I don't dance', and then jumped up smiling to accept the captain, figured so often that she wondered whether there could really be only one villainess.

'No wonder,' they wailed, 'we dare not approach an English girl civilly. We have been snubbed too often.'

She sat on the floor in despair, surrounded by paper, while the kitten played havoc with the heartbroken outpourings of self-pity.

She had answered the first ten letters before she realised what was going to happen.

'Press on regardless,' Elizabeth urged her. 'Send out the comforts to the poor dear boys.'

She lay on her bed, naked, studying an old copy of *Vogue*.

'Do people in London really dress like this?'

She had never been to England.

'Not many,' Lucy said absent-mindedly. 'I only know one,' she added, thinking of Rachel.

'Do you think if I wore my uniform turban back to front, Eleanor would mind? A knot at the back might be more fetching. Or perhaps I should stop wearing it altogether – I'm sure my hair's going dark with all this sweat.'

Elizabeth sat up and shook her hair over her eyes, trying to see it.

Jennifer walked through from the bath-room. The bath water did not run, but Chitti brought up buckets of cold water when required. She sat down at the only looking-glass with her bath-towel round her waist and began to try a silly little white artificial flower at various angles on her head.

'There – do you think? Lucy, do look.'

'What? Oh yes, very sweet.'

'Highly operational,' Elizabeth put in

without looking up.

'Or right at the back?'

'Who are you going out with?'

'Simon.'

'Not the back then – he'd knock it off in no time.'

'Don't speak like that of *my* man.'

'Only speaking highly of his keenness.'

She looked at Lucy suspiciously and moved the flower to the other side. The kitten jumped on her knee and put a paw up to pat her face.

'*My* cat,' she murmured, laying it round her neck. Lucy heard a jeep turn in at the gate and draw up in front of the house.

'There's your man now. You'd better put some clothes on. People don't go out wearing only a kitten muffler, even in Rangoon.'

'I must go like a bomb.'

Jennifer scattered the kitten, the white flower and the bath-towel, and began to race round the room. They heard Greta's voice on the stairs.

'Lucy, tell him I'll be down this instant.'

Jennifer's head struggled out through yards of yellow and white cotton. Lucy stretched her cramped knees and stepped over her fan mail, but at the door she met Greta smiling mysteriously.

'Someone for you, Lucy.'

She rushed the stairs two at a time, not waiting to hear more, and certain of finding

Miles below.

Steve was standing in the sitting-room, looking out across the wet green bushes to the wet green endless scrub beyond. He turned and held out his hands.

'I thought you were Miles.' She was afraid she might be going to cry.

Steve kissed the top of her head.

'Sorry,' he said, 'only me again. Can you come out?'

She backed away and looked at him. His face was browner than ever, and his eyes a more startling, burning blue.

'You look as if you'd been shipwrecked in the tropics and sitting on a raft for days.'

'You look as if you'd got jaundice.'

They both laughed.

'Isn't it lucky,' Steve said, 'that I love you for yourself alone and not for your yellow face?'

'I'm not coining out if you are going to behave tiresomely.'

'Of course I shan't. The soul of propriety and decorum – the marriage of true minds only. After all, we've agreed we both look ghastly.'

'Yes.'

She wasn't too pleased with that. Presumably Miles, when he did come, would also think she looked ghastly. She went upstairs slowly and changed into an evening dress.

Jennifer was still sitting at the glass,

fiddling with her flower. She moved over long enough for Lucy to see that rouge on top of malaria pills was a mistake. She rubbed it off again.

'Is it your husband, Lucy?'

'No, just an old friend.'

'Very smooth?'

She considered this – their highest term of approval.

'I don't know. Aren't you going out to-night?' she asked Elizabeth to divert attention.

'No. Brian's coming here. He's broke and somebody's pinched his jeep anyway.'

Steve and Greta were talking on the window-seat when she came down. Steve got up and took her hand.

'That's better,' he said. 'Though I consider the costume unsuitable for the conditions.'

'Hopelessly unsuitable,' she agreed, 'but it's either this or uniform trousers – can't have bare legs in the evening round here. They get bitten to hell.'

'Look after her,' Greta suddenly smiled at Steve. He smiled back as if they shared some secret.

'I can look after myself.' She felt annoyed at being treated like a child.

'Of course,' Steve said soothingly. 'Good-bye, Mrs. Masters. It's been a pleasure to meet you.'

Greta waved them off from the front

porch, with the spaniel panting at her feet.

'What were you and Greta talking about?'

'This and that. She's a very interesting person. Where do we go to eat in this wilderness?'

'Have you only just come?'

'Flew in yesterday.'

She nearly said 'Why didn't you come yesterday?' but changed it to 'How did you find me?'

'The most notorious lady soldier in the Far East? It wasn't difficult. Told the aircrew I was going to do a story on you – everyone knew where you lived.'

'Well, where are *you* living?'

'In the Press mess.'

'I suppose we'd better eat there then.'

Steve headed the jeep round the top of the airstrip and they began to hurtle towards Rangoon. It was quite dark now and still raining steadily. The pools in the red mud road, which were really potholes, gleamed in the headlights, but it was impossible to avoid them. The jeep swerved and lurched and splashed, and water showered up over the bonnet.

'Was it true, Steve?'

'Was what true?'

'That you were going to do a story on me?'

'Could be – sorry about this, it seems wetter than Cherrapunji.'

'But did you only come for that?'

'What do you think?'

'I think you are an absolute stinker.'

'Why?'

'If you publish anything about me, Miles will divorce me at once.'

'That's rather what I had in mind.'

She could not tell in the light of the rain if he were serious.

'Anyway, you can't.'

'Can't what?'

'Publish anything. Apparently my letter was illegal in the first place.'

'That was only because you had your name in the paper. There's nothing to prevent me circulating the world with "A little lady, 5 feet 3 inches, charming and courageous in every inch, takes up cudgels on behalf of the underdog in S.E. Asia. A member of a certain canteen force in Burma, whose hair is now almost totally black, etc., etc.". Everyone will know who I'm talking about without mentioning names.'

'Oh, please, Steve, you wouldn't?'

'Why not?'

'You couldn't be so mean.'

'How do you know?'

'But I hadn't any idea how much fuss it would cause. It was just a damn fool thing to do and I want to forget all about it.'

'That's going to be hard, honey.' He accelerated cheerfully into the middle of an enormous puddle.

Through dinner he talked about everything in the world except Miles. They ate tinned food and drank canned beer, as if it were lobster and hock. She was still laughing when they walked out to the jeep and found a big moon and no rain.

'Now where?' Steve asked, switching on the engine.

'Could we just drive, and keep driving, very fast?'

'Why not?'

'If you go back past the airstrip there's a fine straight road without potholes because it isn't used all day every day like this one.'

'Where does it lead to?'

'Prome, and the Japanese, but we needn't go that far.'

'That would be an even better story: "War Correspondent and Under-dog girl – suicide pact".'

'But someone else would get the scoop.'

'Never do. Down with the *Mail* and the *Mirror*.'

Beyond Mingaladon the road unwound in the moon, a straight white scarf between silent, dark bushes. She stood up, holding on to the windscreen, and felt the speed increase, sweeping her out of time, out of this world.

'Steve,' she shouted at the top of her voice, 'I'm alive.'

'Didn't you know, darling?'

'I'd forgotten – it's so long since...' Since when?

She pushed away thought – one with the wind, with birds and with angels, her heart breaking with love for the universe.

'Look out,' Steve yelled. 'Hang on – going round this corner.'

He braked and swerved, and she sat down very suddenly, still breathless with ecstasy.

'Where are you going?'

'Thought I'd try this side road.'

'Won't we get lost?'

'Not so far. If we drive straight down here we should be able to drive straight back.'

The road was only a lane leading apparently nowhere till round a small patch of jungly trees they came on the leaden surface of a wide, still lake.

Steve stopped the jeep and they heard the cross voices of a thousand frogs protesting to the moon.

'Somebody used to come here in peace-time. Look.' An old diving-board stuck out above the water and the reeds. Steve ran to the end of it and jumped up and down.

'Pretty mossy now,' he called. 'Shall we bathe?'

'No, thank you. It looks a leech paradise.'

'Here, catch.'

Steve started throwing his things back to her. She caught most of them, but as she stooped to pick up one of his shoes she saw him arch and dive in still wearing his watch. Maybe the reeds and mud are thick close to the surface, who knows how long ago someone dived there...

'Your watch, you fool,' she shouted to him in a voice sharp with anxiety when his head appeared again.

'Waterproof,' he shouted back. 'Come on in – it's deliciously cool.'

But she was angry still and went and sat in the jeep smoking one of his cigarettes to discourage mosquitoes, and glowering at the sky. He joined her in about ten minutes. He had put on his shoes and his trousers.

'God, that was wonderful. I feel terrific.'

'You won't feel so good when the mosquitoes get to work on that manly chest.'

'Hey, what's biting you?'

'Nothing – nothing at all.'

'But, honey, what's wrong with bathing on a hot night?' He looked genuinely puzzled.

'You never even tried the water to see if it was more than a foot deep.'

'But if it had been shallow I'd only have gone in an awful flop.'

'You might have been killed.'

She folded governess hands in her lap, but Steve flung his arms round her.

'Adorable Lucy, thank you for worrying about me.'

His skin was cool and she rubbed her cheek against it for a second before she drew away.

'Of course I worried. I wasn't going in there to drag you out by the feet, and how would it have looked if I'd brought the jeep back empty?'

'Leave it at that then. I'm undrowned and very resilient.'

He reversed rapidly into the mud, turned and bumped off towards the main road again. Twenty yards from it he suddenly drove into the scrub at the side and switched off the lights and the engine.

'Sh – what was that?'

'I don't hear anything.'

'Sounded like a tank on the main road.'

'Couldn't be – at night,' but now she too could hear a whirring rattle unlike any lorry, coming nearer. They were under a big tree, protected from the moon. Steve put his arm round her shoulders.

'Whatever it is,' he said cheerfully, 'it's coming from Rangoon, so it must be one of ours, and there is no reason why it should turn down here, anyway.'

'No, Steve.'

They sat very still watching the end of the lane.

'Of course it's ours,' Steve whispered as the first half of the tank appeared shining in the moon. It was travelling fast, but it seemed to take a long time to cross their line of vision. A coop of squawking chickens was tied inexplicably to the back.

'I think we'll wait a few minutes.' Steve's voice sounded uncertain. She could not see his face.

'May be more of them, and I don't want to be cut in half barging out of a side road.'

They waited in silence. She lay back against Steve's arm and wished she was safe in England with Miles, preferably eating an apple in front of a roaring wood fire. She shivered at the delightful idea.

'Are you cold?'

'No, not a bit. Just wishing I was.'

'White Christmas stuff all the boys moan for?'

'Yes – snow seems so appetising – crisp, brilliant.'

'Slush and mud in London.'

'Maybe we shan't live in London.'

'Where then?'

'I don't know yet. It depends what Miles wants to do. He was only just qualified before the war.'

Steve's hand came up gently into her hair.

'Lucy...'

'Just here.'

'Do I come into your sunny, snowy, future at all?'

'Of course not. You're just an accident.'

'Strictly hostilities only?'

'But in peace you'd never stay in one place. You'd be all over the world on the track of the little wars, and Miles and I are going to settle down. You couldn't possibly go on being a friend of ours.'

'I don't want to be a friend of Miles. Come to that, I don't want to be a friend of yours either.'

His hand tightened on her hair.

'Let go, Steve. You're hurting.'

'You're hurting me, too.'

His face was only a grey blur where the moon filtered through the leaves. She would not believe in and support his sorrow.

'It's not true.'

She faced him fiercely. 'You've got hundreds of women and you don't give a damn for any of them, and you never noticed me till I was safely provided for. You're playing a game with yourself to do down Miles, or make me do something stupid for a good newspaper story.'

It was only because of the bloody war and the bloody heat that she had to find herself alone with an angry and attractive man in the middle of the night.

'I hate you, I hate you.'

The tears streamed down her face. 'Of course it was a Japanese tank, the British don't keep hens, and now you take advantage of the whole situation to make me mind about you drowning in the mud.' She beat her fists on his chest. 'I wish you had drowned – it would have done you good.

Think you've only got to lift your little finger and surround people with Japanese soldiers and you can take advantage of anyone...'

Steve's arms closed round her.

'Darling – stop talking like a novelette. You won't get any advantages taken of you, no such luck for either of us. I happen to love you so I shan't be treating you badly – unless you badly want to be treated badly?'

She laid her head against him and closed her eyes, she felt too tired to live.

'No, thank you,' she said faintly.

'Speak up. I can't hear with my heart.'

'No,' she shouted, raising her head which was a mistake.

'Too loud for the Japanese look-outs,' he whispered as he kissed her. She clung to him, desperately, drowning together in the last flood.

'But I love Miles,' she said as soon as she could speak. 'I'm sure I love him. I don't understand anything.'

'It's all right, sweetheart.' Steve rocked her gently, soothing her. 'It's all right, of course you do. This is a night out of time, to be forgotten.'

He took one arm away and started the engine.

'I'm driving you home now, Japs or no Japs. We've stayed out too late.'

He edged the jeep forward on to the road.

There was nothing coming in either direction. She still lay against him, not moving; he stroked her hair and her ear and from time to time kissed her on the forehead.

At the front door he drove the jeep in under the porch. The Ghurka guard at the gate jumped up and saluted, and then turned his back on them.

'Home, Lucy.'

She did not want to look up. She was still heavy with unexplained despair.

'Darling, you've got to get out now. Go upstairs, climb into bed, lie down and fall fast asleep and forget this evening ever existed. I shan't see you again.'

'Not ever?'

'Not for a long time, anyway.'

'But, Steve, I want the moon *and* the stars. I don't know what's happened.'

She still could not leave go of him. The earth beyond the compass of his body was no longer solid.

'Don't make it worse for me, darling.'

She could no longer doubt the pain in his voice. She drew away and stumbled out.

'Lucy...'

'Yes, love?'

'Kiss me good-bye, darling.'

Holding her dress up over the puddles in the drive, she walked slowly round to his side of the jeep. She kissed him with chaste sorrow as if he were in a hospital bed, and she one of twenty ward visitors. He began to laugh and they kissed again, laughing, whispering, with a desert island around them.

'Where do you live in London?'

'I don't know.'

'Well, where did you? You have to start from somewhere.'

She gave him Miles's mother's address, and Rachel's.

'But you couldn't come to either of those places, really. There isn't any future, this was just one great big *feu de joie* of a mistake.'

'Not enough *feu* for me, or *joie* either. Good-bye, love of my life, look after yourself.'

He switched on the lights.

'Now there's no time and I should have told you–'

'No, don't, you'll be sorry later. "Whatever made me say those silly things to that man – what was his names, Miles? You remember, the tall thin one. It must have been the heat."'

'Don't darling, don't – even if it's never true again it's true tonight. Let me say it. Please.'

'Shan't listen – no need for both of us to make anything irrevocable. Good-bye.'

The jeep suddenly sprang away from her and he was gone, leaving her standing like Isolde with her hands stretched out, pleading to a warm, blank darkness.

She took off her shoes and crept upstairs. Both the other girls were veiled in white mosquito-nets. Across the room, she heard Jennifer snoring, and in the moonlight saw a lizard zigzag up the wall. She went through her snake routine mechanically, but her bed was empty of menace.

Chapter Fifteen

'Saw you out with an officer last night.'

The flight sergeant leant on the counter accusingly.

'Last night? Oh, that wasn't an officer, that was a war correspondent.'

'Got a jeep of his own anyway – saw you tearing round the top of the strip. Have a good time?'

'Yes, thank you.'

'Better than you had at *our* do, I suppose?'

'Oh, Frankie, don't keep on at me. Of course I enjoyed your do.'

'Been more fun with officers present though, wouldn't it?'

'Listen, Frankie, I shall crown you with the tea urn in a minute. Last night was the first time I've spent the evening alone with anyone who had a jeep since I came to Burma. He happened to be a chap I've known for a long time who was just passing through. Of course I wanted to see him just for a few hours.'

'Sorry, Lucy. It gets me all het up and then the boys in the mess tell such awful stories, they're a lot of scum the things they say I know, but it kind of gets under your skin...'

'What things do they say?'

'I'd rather not tell you.'

'Go on. You're longing to.'

'Well, only that any chap with money to burn can go down to your mess any night and have a good time – you know what I mean?'

'Yes, I know what you mean all right. How much money do they suggest is necessary?'

'Len said thirty-five chips...'

'Frankie, how could you listen? You've been round to our place often enough for a meal yourself.'

'I know it's not true really. I know you all, Lucy. I know none of you mean any harm, but when I'm with the boys it all looks different. There aren't enough of you – we all get steamed up – and then when I saw you with that officer last night I thought you'd been laughing at us all the time, anyway. I was nearly off my chump, I can tell you. I went on a blind last night. I feel awful.'

'Are you flying today?'

'Not till this afternoon.'

'Go and have a long, cold bath.'

'Right-o, Lucy... I say, no offence taken, I hope?'

She felt cold with despair and failure and tired to the roots of her hair.

'No, Frankie, no offence taken.'

'Look, couldn't you get Eleanor to give you the jeep tonight?'

'You know she never lets any of us touch it.'

'Pity. I could have taken you up to the pictures at Two Div. They're showing "The Way Ahead".'

'It's a kind thought. They're sending a truck for us anyway, thanks. Look, Frankie, come in to supper tomorrow night, bring Len, and we'll show him what really goes on.'

'Wizard show. Be seeing you.'

He slouched out with his bush hat on the back of his head. There goes, she thought, one of our friends. There are approximately forty-seven thousand men in the district who know us by sight only. It is unlikely that their gossip is any more kindly. We are not dispensing carbo-hydrates and char and encouragement – we are spreading envy, malice, lust and backbiting. Elizabeth is going dark to no purpose, Jennifer should be lounging at home in the hills with a cheetah, Eleanor need not have prickly heat, Greta could be with her husband in the town, and I with Miles in Madras, in which case last night would never have happened.

She rubbed the sweat off her forehead with her rolled-up sleeve.

'You all right, Lucy?'

'Yes, thanks, Joe.'

'You look a bit queer.'

'Feeling the heat.'

'Out late too, weren't you?'

'How do you know?'

'Passed you on the Prome road in my truck.'

She did not ask what time; defence, was not worth while. By this evening, several thousand idle men with not enough to do would have torn the flesh off her bones and consigned her to the gutter.

'Was that your husband, Lucy?'

'Who, Bill?' as if she didn't know.

'The tall chap you were out with last night.'

'No such luck.'

'Funny, sounded from what Derek said...'

'And what did Derek say?'

'Nothing much – only saw you laughing in Rangoon.'

'And what's wrong with laughing?'

'Nothing, Lucy, nothing. Calm down, girl, don't bite my head off. Glad somebody's got something to laugh at in this blistering mud-hole. What wouldn't I give for a pint of good bitter at the Dog and Duck.'

In a way it made everything easier. She could hate Steve who had flown in, landed her in all this, and taken off again for more convenient climates. But where had he gone?

'Char, please, Lucy. Day-dreaming?'

'What? Sorry, Jim – no, what did you say?'

'Let's have some char, ducks.'

'Where's your mug?'

'I lost it, please, miss.'

'You know we haven't got any mugs. You all pinched them.'

'Oh, go on, be a sport, give us it in a fruit tin.'

'You'll cut yourself.'

'Not nimble Jim – he knows how to look after himself, like some others we know, eh, Lucy?'

'I don't know what you mean.'

'Now, now, not up on your high horse. Where was Private Spender when the dawn came up like thunder?'

That was one hour.

She was nearly through to the end of the third hour when she lost her temper.

'Good-looker, wasn't he, Lucy?'

The face, propped on elbows across the counter, leered hopefully.

'Oh, for heaven's sake, Taffy, why pick on me? All the girls go out to dinner.'

She was uncertain whether she was going to cry, faint, or go screaming mad.

'Aha.' Taffy waggled a finger at her. 'But we all thought you were different.'

'Well, I'm not,' she snapped.

She turned and walked out of the canteen without waiting for the relief shift or the truck, leaving the cakes uncounted and the cash in the toffee tin, and a row of astonished, open pink mouths in nut-brown faces.

She stumped up the airstrip, splashing deliberately in the standing pools. She pulled off her stuffy green turban and her hair fell down to her shoulders. Let them pour their own filthy tea, let Chitti pinch the cash and the airmen the gramophone records, she would probably be the first member of the ladylike W.C.F. to be court-martialled.

'Did you or did you not, Private Spender, on the 25th ult., abandon your post of duty?'

'I did.'

'Leaving valuable Army property un-attended?'

'That is correct.'

'You are unable to produce any reason for this unpredictable behaviour?'

'I was out of my mind.'

'That is not just cause...'

'It's an impediment.'

'Prisoner at the dock, do not interrupt counsel.'

'Lucy...' She started guiltily.

'Oh, hallo, Joe.' She walked on, staring sullenly at the mud.

'Listen, don't mind the boys. They didn't mean it.'

'Oh, didn't they?'

'Everyone's very cut up about it.'

'Oh, they are, are they?'

'Lucy, listen. You'll get into trouble going off like that.'

'I seem to be in trouble, anyway.'

'Don't do anything silly – just for a bit of teasing. Come on back now.'

'No, thank you.'

'Well, look, if you won't come back, get in my truck and I'll run you home and we'll tell them you felt ill. Taffy's holding the fort at the canteen. I've briefed him to say that anyway if your captain shows up.'

'Oh, help, Joe. Eleanor's on the next shift.'

She stood stockstill in a puddle with her hand to her mouth. Joe went on patiently:

'That's what I thought. Now hop in, here's my truck. Trust the R.A.F. We'll have you out of this with no damage done.'

She climbed up into the truck. Her legs felt weak and old.

'Found a snake in the works yesterday,' Joe said, trying to make conversation.

'It's gone now though?' She closed her eyes.

'Rather, it was dead anyway, poor brute – a long one, about five foot.'

'I don't like snakes.'

Snakes in the grass, snakes in the tent, snakes under the bed and in the works, and yesterday Chitti brought a small snake into the sitting-room—very small, and laid it at Eleanor's feet, dead and dull, saying: 'Very bad snake.' She climbed slowly out of the truck at the front door. Eleanor was waiting for her.

'Private Spender fainted,' Joe said with a hand under her arm for the steps.

'Poor Lucy.' Eleanor was worried and sorry and hurried her up to bed after thanking Joe.

'Now don't get up till I come back from the canteen anyway. Are you sure you are all right now? You aren't feverish?'

Lucy assured her that she was not feverish.

'Oh, by the way,' Eleanor said at the door. 'Something to cheer you up before I go. Mrs. Bannister was over here this morning and she's decided to promote you after all. Bye-bye, Corporal.'

Lucy turned her face to the wall and waited to go off her head.

Chapter Sixteen

At last the telegram came:

'Must see you – hope soon – Miles.'

'Do you think he would have sent it, Greta, if he was going straight to Japan?'

'Of course not – expect he's on his way here now.'

'I wish I knew when. I'm sure I'll be out when he arrives.'

'Never mind. If he's posted here, you'll have plenty of time together. Eleanor's very good about that sort of thing.'

'How can you knit in this climate? It makes me hot to look at you.'

'My daughter's having her first baby in Aberdeen this winter. I must knit something. It's the smallest garment I could find.'

She held up a very tiny vest.

'I expect it'll be a very small baby.'

Lucy tried to sound polite.

'Her husband's enormous,' Greta said, 'and she's five-foot ten herself, so I confidently expect the baby to be huge too, but I'm only showing willing.'

She started to count stitches again, and Lucy, restless and unsettled, wandered out to the veranda, but the smell of drains was too strong and she came in and went up-stairs, only to find Elizabeth at the dressing-table doing the canteen accounts in a big ledger.

'What's thirty-seven rupees and fifty-nine annas?' she asked, naked and distracted, so Lucy left quickly. In the dining-room she poured herself a glass of real lime juice, a luxury beyond price. They had found a little sack of fresh limes thrown in with their normal ration of tins last week. She rolled it round her tongue, so much more invigorating than vitamin pills, and, walked reluctantly up to the garage to check stores, a job she had never liked doing alone since the day she found the scorpion behind the Sunlight soap.

After a time she sat down on a crate of tinned pineapple and pulled out Miles's telegram again. There was no date or time on it so perhaps he was already on his way. By sea five days, by air a few hours, so it could be tonight or next week. She jumped up and ran back into the house, calling to Chitti to bring hot water. She had an hour to wash her hair before her shift at the canteen.

'It won't dry.' Elizabeth looked up from her rupees.

'Oh, it must, it must.'

Lucy hung her head out of the window and shook it wildly to and fro.

'I should have bleached it again. Have you any peroxide?'

'No.'

'Damn everything. I haven't seen him for months, I look ghastly. I wish I hadn't taken the malaria pills.'

'Why, Lucy, you're acting like a bomb. What's come over you?'

'What can I do?'

She stopped in front of the glass, but Elizabeth's head was as usual in the way. From what she could see of her face it was lined, hollow, yellow, with bags under the eyes. Her lank, dark, wet hair added to the general impression of a middle-aged witch.

'I shall die, just die.' She flung herself down on her bed, but death eluded her.

'Your hair will dry even less that way,' Elizabeth pointed out. 'Why don't you go to bed early? That always helps...'

'To bring the buttercups back into the cheeks? I could tonight, actually. 207's party is Thursday, tomorrow there's that ship. Tonight I'll go to bed at eight. I really will.'

She sprang up, alive again and waved her head out of the window at the sun.

By seven-thirty, after the normal panic caused by three women changing to go out, Lucy and Elizabeth were alone in the house, along with the Ghurka guard and Nelly, the spaniel. They had both put on dressing-gowns and were finishing plates of tinned pineapple when they heard a truck on the drive.

'Oh, damn.' Elizabeth banged her spoon in her pineapple juice with a splash. 'And I wanted to go to bed early too.'

Lucy went to the door.

'Good evening,' said the sailor, 'I've called to collect the party for H.M.S. – I was told six girls.'

'Oh, no.' Lucy looked at him as if he were a messenger from the underworld. 'That's tomorrow, surely?'

'No, miss, tonight. I should have been here half an hour ago, only I lost my way in the lanes out here.'

'Do come in.'

Lucy thought feverishly. It had certainly never been a party of six. Who had promised to go? Not Greta, not Eleanor, it must have been Jennifer and Elizabeth.

'There's been an awful mistake,' she told him. 'We were all looking forward to it so much, but we thought it was tomorrow, and there are only two of us here tonight as you can see.'

She waved an arm at Elizabeth behind her in the dining-room Elizabeth was making frantic signals of one about to fall asleep. Lucy ignored her.

'If two would be better than none, we could be ready in a quarter of an hour.'

'Well, frankly, miss,' said the sailor, 'they'd kill me dead if I turned up at the ship without anyone.'

'Come on, Elizabeth, such fun, we're going to a party.' She ran upstairs without looking back, knowing that Elizabeth would follow her anyway in order to argue

'Lucy, you're the limit. I won't come, why should I?'

'We'll go to bed early tomorrow. You were going to come then.'

'But I don't like sailors.'

'Nonsense. Every nice girl...'

'I'm not nice then, and my feet are killing me.'

'So are mine. Look, it won't be bad, honestly. It's in the wardroom. No dancing.'

Elizabeth brightened and began to change with maddening slowness.

'That's just as well,' she said. 'I couldn't stand tonight, let alone dance.' She slipped off her dressing-gown. 'I know,' she suggested, 'let's just tell him to go away.'

'No.' Lucy was firm with her. 'We said we'd go and we are going, and you and I have got to be gay for six.'

She left Elizabeth groaning and ran down to tell the sailor they were nearly ready.

But it was a long, slow journey into Rangoon. The sailor was not accustomed to driving by night through a blinding downpour. Twice in the town he lost the way and again in the darkened docks among the rubble. It was after nine o'clock when he delivered them at the wardroom of the cruiser.

'Hullo there,' said the captain, coming forward with a tumbler of gin in one hand, 'we'd given you up hours ago. Where are the others?'

Lucy explained. She was relieved to see they were supported by three jolly nursing sisters.

'Been trying to keep our spirits up. So sad you couldn't come.' The first lieutenant also seemed to be drinking gin by the half-pint.

'Food's all gone – did you proud.' He waved sadly at the empty plates.

'Let's get out of this,' Elizabeth hissed.

'Can't,' Lucy whispered back. 'Transport laid on at 11 p.m.'

She began to edge over towards the nurses with an idea of making a solid phalanx of sobriety, but the nearest nurse glared at her rather squintly, and she saw they had paired off with the three most attractive officers and also held large glasses of gin.

'Like to see my cabin?' asked the first lieutenant. 'Jolly interesting.' He stooped in order to look her in the eye.

'No, thank you.'

'Show you the engines, then?'

'Hey, Jimmy, that's my job.'

'Didn't see you, Sparks. Tell you what,

both go – make a party.'

'I haven't got a drink.' It might be easier to bear if one were not so sober with such wet feet.

'No drink? It's a crime. What were you thinking of, Sparks? Fetch the lady a drink – what's your name? Lucy – bring Lucy Locket's friend with you. We'll go on, won't we, Lucy?'

'I'll just wait for my friend.'

'What's the idea?' Elizabeth, furious at her side.

'We are going round the ship.'

'Oh God, what for?'

'To keep them on the move – they may fall downstairs and break their darling necks.'

Elizabeth giggled and the tour began. No. 1, Lucy, Sparks, Elizabeth, in single file, along narrow corridors, through steel hatches, up and down steep ladders into the hot heart of the ship.

'There,' said the chief engineer triumphantly. He flung open an enormous oven door and they glimpsed the fiery furnace within.

'You must use a lot of coal,' Lucy commented politely. 'Particularly at sea.'

Sparks thought this remark so funny that he very nearly fell into the furnace himself.

'That's good,' he roared. 'That's great. I like that. Hear that, boys?'

He included the gloomy band of silent

stokers, who allowed a small smile to creep across their disapproving faces.

'Coal,' he roared three ladders farther up. 'I like that, it's bloody good. Wait till I tell the Old Man.'

He hurried them back into the wardroom. Lucy found herself imprisoned by hot, red and laughing mouths.

'Three cheers for the miner's daughter,' a voice shouted.

She was seized from behind and swung up on to the table. She stood there, stupidly, still holding her untouched drink, her slippery clean hair had fallen forward across one eye.

'"Oh, my darling Clementine",' they sang, all swaying towards her, all their faces wide open, the air heavy with gin and smoke. Somebody pushed a large shoe into her free hand.

A flashlight suddenly exploded. She noticed for the first time an American in the corner by the nurses, wearing a camera as big as a barrel organ. Oh God, oh God, she thought, it can't be true. What have I ever done to deserve this?

She jumped down, helped by six eager hands and pushed her way through to the photographer. The fatal words 'War Correspondent' were written on his sleeve.

'Oh, please, you won't use that one?'

'Me – use what?'

'That photograph you just took.'

'Lady, cross my heart, I'm not here on business. Just loosed off a light to make the party go.'

'Honest?'

'Sure, sure. Why should I waste my time that way?'

She gave up. There might be hope or there might not. There was still half an hour of this nightmare to go. Elizabeth yawned openly.

'What's the matter with your friend, Lucy? Got no life in her.'

'We all work quite hard in the daytime.'

'Don't kid me, you girls have a whale of a time – one long party.'

'Come on, Lucy, give us a song.'

'I can't sing.'

'Make your friend sing – she hasn't said a thing all evening. Anyone would think she was at a funeral. Cheer up, Dismal Daisy.'

'My name's Elizabeth – *if* you please.'

'Sorry I spoke, I'm sure. What's eating you? Look at the nurses, good girls, laughing their heads off.'

'So I see.'

'Have another drink – all have another drink.'

'No, thank you. Lucy, isn't it time to go?'

'Nearly.'

'Go? Who's talking about going? Night's as young as a new-born lamb, and you haven't seen my cabin yet.'

'We are leaving in ten minutes, I'm afraid.'

'No, no, you're not. Somebody's blundered – no question of it. Come on, let's go and see my pin-ups.'

'No, thank you' – crossed ankles and folded hands and faces of despairing primness.

'Lucy, there's our sailor – the one who brought us.'

'Where?'

'In a doorway, talking to the captain.'

'Why, hullo, young ladies. I was just telling Able Seaman Jackson here that you won't need transport yet awhile.'

'I'm afraid we must go. It's been very kind of you, but our captain doesn't allow us to stay out late.'

'I'll square your captain. Leave it to me. She's young and pretty too, I take it?'

'No, really, thank you very much. As a matter of fact, my friend doesn't feel very well – she had her appendix out last week.'

Lying desperately and continuously, they fought a rearguard action to the gangway where they turned and ran waving, with safety in sight, at the cheering officers along the rails.

'This way, miss.'

'Oh, we were so pleased to see you. What's your other name?'

'Jack – Jack Jackson.'

'We were really getting very sleepy. It was stuffy in there, and then when we thought the captain was sending you away again...'

'Come back *much* later, he said.'

'Wait for me.' The American photographer joined them out of the dark.

'You going through Rangoon?'

'That's right, sir.'

'Drop me off someplace, will you?'

Lucy climbed into the front of the truck by Jackson and Elizabeth and the American got in behind. There was a long, exhausted silence. The truck twisted and bumped through the deserted city of dreadful night. It was after curfew time, and no one moved in the streets or slipped through the shadows of the ruins. Lucy shut her eyes and tried a few stanzas of Gray's Elegy. Its soothing properties were spoilt, however, by an irritated squeak from the back of the truck.

'Oh, really, do behave yourself.' Elizabeth's voice always became more Sloane Street in anger. There was a scuffle and a sharp slap. Jackson stopped the truck without looking round.

'Perhaps the other young lady would like to come in front too,' he suggested.

Lucy held out a hand, and Elizabeth climbed over.

'Thank you, Jack. *Some people...*' she said.

She unwound her dress from the gears, but could not find words strong enough to finish her sentence.

'Say, what's the idea?' The American leaned over the front seat. 'Don't you like me?'

'No,' Elizabeth said. 'Not one little tiny bit.'

'For Chris' sake what's the matter with you English girls? Frigid, the lot of you. What's wrong with a bit of necking? What do you think you're out for in this goddam country?'

The girls said nothing.

'What's the matter? Lost your tongues? No manners and no sex appeal, that's what's the matter. What about a bit of comfort for the boys who are killing themselves for you? Who do you think you are anyway? Queen Victoria? How long do you think those poor bastards have been at sea? Why didn't you go on deck and give the boys a break? Blocks of goddam ice ... couple of bloody ice-boxes. Talk about chilled meat...'

Jackson stopped the truck again.

'This is where you get out, sir,' he said, in a voice without expression.

'The hell I do. I'm going all the way with the girls. I'm going to show them–'

'This is your stop, sir,' Jackson repeated mulishly.

'Stop? What d'yer mean, stop?'

'You wanted to get out here to meet your friends.'

The girders of a bombed warehouse drooped in the moonlight.

'Did I? Did I say that?'

'That's right, sir, your friends and the other girls.' Jackson came round and held open the door.

'What girls?'

'Dancing girls,' Jackson replied with a poker face. The American stumbled out on to the road.

'Say, what's the idea? I don't see any girls.' He waved his head from side to side like a tortoise.

'Along in a minute,' Jackson called as he started up the engine. 'They're off to meet the wizard,' he bellowed in a sudden burst of hilarity. The girls joined in. They looked back to see the American run a few steps after them shaking his fist and then fall flat in the middle of the road.

'The wizard, the wonderful wizard,' they shouted with relief. Elizabeth beat Jackson on the back.

'Up the Navy,' she said and started '"Every nice girl loves a sailor",' of her own accord.

'I'm sorry I couldn't hit him,' Jackson said as he brought them to the door of their house. 'I'd have liked to knock his teeth down his throat.'

'You were marvellous,' Lucy told him. 'I'll never forget the way you said "dancing girls".'

'Wish I could have done more. If it hadn't been for the wife and kids I'd have knocked him cold, officer or no officer, damn Yank – talking about our girls like that.'

'Now then, Jack, mustn't insult the Allies.'

'And what was he doing, I'd like to know?' He grinned and shook hands all round.

'I don't think,' Elizabeth whispered as she walked into the house, 'I've ever been so tired since the day I was born. Someone's still up – light on in the sitting-room.'

'I'm going straight to bed!' Lucy had her foot on the bottom stair when Greta called out:

'Is that you, Lucy? Wherever have you been?'

She came back reluctantly and stood blinking in the lamplight. Greta was not alone.

'Oh, no,' Lucy said, and found she had spoken aloud. Miles stood up and came over to her, but he was not smiling. He kissed her on the cheek.

'Well, darling?' It was a demand for an explanation.

'We went to a party.'

'Mrs. Masters said you were staying in to-night.'

'Yes, I was, I was going to bed early,' a hundred years ago. 'But we got the night wrong for the cruiser.'

'What *have* you been doing? You're covered with mud.'

'Am I?'

'Yes. Look at your dress and your hair's been dragged through a bush backwards.'

'I washed it.'

Washed it this morning for you – two hundred years ago.

'I thought you'd understand I was coming soon from my cable.'

'I thought "soon" might mean anything.'

'I've only got tonight and tomorrow.'

'Oh, Miles? What then?'

'Back to India.'

'To India...' she echoed stupidly. 'What for?'

Greta got up.

'I'll say good night now. You two will have a lot to say to each other.'

They hardly saw her go. Lucy took her place on the window-seat and Miles sat down again beside her.

'I don't understand, Miles. I thought you were going to Japan?'

'Whatever made you think that? I've come to see you.'

'You've got some leave?'

'Not exactly – well, yes, compassionate leave if you want to know.'

'What for?'

'I was worried about you.'

'But I'm quite safe here, Miles. The Japanese are way up-country now, it's as safe as living in London – safer. There aren't any bombs. We are really very comfortable here, with a roof over our heads, and you can see how nice Eleanor has made it with chair covers and things...' Her voice trailed off at the look on his face. 'Miles, what's the matter?'

'Don't you honestly know?'

'No, I haven't a clue. Darling, what is it?'

'Damn it, Lucy, you *must* know. I sometimes wonder whether you aren't a screw loose somewhere. You must know that people are talking about you, my wife, all over India? You might at least have kept my name out of it,' he ended miserably with his eyes on his highly-polished shoes.

Light exploded in her tired brain.

'Oh – the letter – you were worried about the silly old letter. It was rather a mistake, but it didn't really matter, they've promoted me just the same. They overlooked it. I'm a corporal now.'

'They overlooked it. Lucy, you don't understand anything. Everywhere I go people say "Spender? Any relation to that hot piece in Burma? Your wife. I say, old chap, better keep an eye on her".'

'Oh – just because I like dancing proper steps, instead of being marched straight round a room?'

'Jesus Christ, it seemed as simple as that to you?'

'Yes. Oh, Miles, please, it's so long since

260

we saw each other, do we have to waste all the time quarrelling?'

'I'm not quarrelling with you. I'm just trying to remind you I'm there.'

'But, darling, I'm always thinking about you.'

'You don't think constructively.'

'But I can't see why it's upset you.'

A jeep stopped at the front door and Miles stood up again.

'That's a chap coming to fetch me. I'm staying in his mess.'

'But aren't you staying here?'

'Of course not.'

'But when are we going to see each other?'

'My plane leaves at five tomorrow afternoon.'

'But I shall be working.'

'Perhaps Mrs. Masters will give you some time off.'

'But even if she does, Miles, it's so little, only a few hours.'

'We should be able to straighten things out in a few hours, if we both try hard.'

An R.A.M.C. captain came forward and introduced himself as Taylor.

'Don't want to hurry you, Spender, but it's already an hour later than we agreed.'

'I'm quite ready. Good night, Lucy.'

'Oh, Miles.'

'Now don't do anything silly,' he whispered as Taylor tactfully turned his back and went out to the jeep. Lucy fought down hysteria and returned his half-hearted kiss.

'I'll try to do the first shift,' she said, 'and be free from ten o'clock. Come then if you can. We'll have lunch here.'

When the sound of the jeep died away she was still sitting on the bottom stair. How many stairs? At least ten, then the bend and ten more, and for each stair how many muscles in the knee, the calf, the thigh? She sat with her elbows on her knees, her head in her hands, the mud-stains on her pink linen dress made an irregular brown pattern; fingers, open across her eyes, barred the checks of the red-tiled floor. The Ghurka guard snored on the doorstep, lying uncomfortably on his gun.

'Lucy–' Greta's whisper over the stairs.

'Hullo?'

'Has he gone?'

'Yes.'

'Don't forget to turn out the lamps, dear.'

'No. Greta – will you change shifts with me tomorrow?'

'Certainly. Will you be awake for the early shift do you think?'

'Oh yes.'

Since there was no question of sleep there could be no question of not waking. She put out one hurricane lamp in the sitting-room and carrying the other attempted, the stairs. This is my oxygen mask, can it last to the summit? Each stair hacked out with effort in solid ice. Half-way a ledge to rest, breath coming in shallow gasps. Ten more stairs to go. She looked up to see Greta's startled eyes over the banisters.

'What's wrong, dear?'

'Nothing, just a bit tired. It's been a long evening.' A long day, a long life, a long way to go to the tomb. But here was a grave, a shroud, enveloping clouds of horrid white organdie. She struggled through the mosquito-net to her pillow and fell face downwards on her bed, stunned with sleep, the muddy folds of linen still covering her ankles.

Chapter Seventeen

Miles came into the canteen at a quarter to ten.

'Got a lift to the strip,' he explained.

Lucy was aware of curious eyes raised over tin mugs all round the canteen. Miles sat down at an empty table opposite her. He drummed on the cloth and looked at his watch. She muddled the change and dropped a sausage roll into somebody's tea.

'Steady on, Lucy. I take sugar in *my* char. I'm funny that way.'

'What you beefing about, Nobby? Got it buckshee, didn't you?'

'I say, old man, whatever shall I do? I left my fishing-rod up at the old shooting-box – ra, ra.'

'Get your head down, Nobby. Get your teeth into it.'

Lucy removed the roll with a couple of spoons and threw away the crumby tea.

'What's the matter with her this morning? All of a tremble, girl. More late nights?'

Behind her she heard, thankfully, Greta's cheerful arrival. Miles followed her out to the truck.

'You aren't going to drive that yourself?'

264

'Yes, why not? Our driver's in hospital. It's not far. Don't you trust me?'

She banged the door and forced the gear savagely forward. Miles folded his arms.

'What did you say?' she asked.

'Nothing.'

'Oh – thought you did. This thing makes such a noise.'

'It wouldn't if you changed gear more smoothly.'

'Oh, Miles, what's the matter with you?'

'What did you say?'

'What's the matter?'

'What?'

'Oh hell, never mind.'

She led Miles into the empty house.

Eleanor had gone to Rangoon, taking with her the last chance of borrowing the jeep even for a few hours. Jennifer and Elizabeth were out with the mobile canteen.

'We can stay here for a bit and play the gramophone.'

'Whatever for?'

'I thought you might like it.'

'I haven't come several thousand miles to wind up a gramophone.'

'I'll do the winding.' She knelt on the floor and began to turn the handle.

'Don't be silly, Lucy. I want to talk to you.'

'But you talked to me last night. What more can you have to say?'

'Plenty. I want to go into the whole subject

thoroughly. I want to know how you came to do such a thing, so that we can work out together some way of preventing you acting like that again.'

She was frowning at a blue record label.

'Oh, I shan't ever, I promise you. They told me afterwards it wasn't allowed – really. I never want to write to the papers again as long as we both do live. Shall I put on the last movement of Chopin's Piano Concerto?'

'Lucy, listen to me...' He caught her wrist and the record shattered on the red tiles between them.

'Oh dear, now look what you've done, and it's Eleanor's record – she'll be furious.'

'Blast the record. Do try and concentrate. It isn't just letters to the papers. Goodness knows what you mightn't think up next to humiliate me.'

'But I don't mean to humiliate you.'

'I know you don't, but you never stop to think for one second of the result of any of your follies...'

'You talk as if I was running a leg show.'

'You certainly manage to turn yourself into a cheap vaudeville act. I thought you did regret making a fool of yourself in India and you were going to start growing up and living like a normal adult. In fact, I thought I had some influence over you...'

'But you have. I told you, I think about you nearly all the time. Miles, you haven't even kissed me yet.'

'I don't feel like kissing you at the moment. I'm too angry.'

'You look so handsome when you're angry – please.'

'Lucy, for the last time, will you solemnly promise me to stay out of trouble till we can be together again?'

'Of course I'll promise, but what do you call trouble?'

Miles put his head in his hands.

'I wish to God I knew. If I could imagine what you were going to do I could easily tell you not to.'

'Do you think we should have a picnic lunch?' she asked. Miles looked up again.

'But where could we go?'

'Just down the lane a bit into the country.'

'Looks more like jungle to me.'

'Please, Miles, otherwise all the others will be here for lunch. Please, do kiss me and say I'm forgiven, really I won't do it again, whatever it might be.'

They walked single file down the narrow path, saying nothing. Miles's clean shoes were covered with red mud; he carried the picnic, Lucy slipped about behind him, the mud welled inside her sandals, squeezing between her bare toes.

'Where do you propose to sit down?' Miles asked.

She looked in vain for a grassy bank, a mossy log.

'Up a tree, perhaps,' she suggested wildly. Miles did not even answer. Over a slight rise they came to a ruined factory, already overgrown, once the reason for the path, which once was a road. They sat on a pile of stones eating sausage rolls.

'Have you seen any interesting diseases lately?'

'Only variations of amoebic dysentery.'

'How many nurses are in love with you?'

'None, I should think. They have a wide choice.'

'I'm sure none of the other doctors are so good-looking, though.'

'I don't know about that. You'll get hookworm if you often go about in those open sandals.'

'I'll send you a cable when I do.'

'I shan't be able to get this sort of leave again. Someone else will have to cure you.'

Four hours now till his plane went. Fear and desperation choked her, the sausage stuck in her throat. There must be a passage somewhere through the ice-floes to the promised land.

'How can we get to know each other in a few hours?' she broke out.

'But I know you very well.'

'You don't – and I know nothing about you, and now we never shall.'

'Lucy, you're exaggerating as usual. We shall have years and years together after the war.'

'After the war. How do you know there will ever be anything after today? This is all we are sure of.'

She laid her arm on his with a violent gesture which spilt his beer on his well-creased trousers. She rocked back on her heels, biting her lip while, with steady deliberation, he took out a spotless handkerchief and mopped his knee.

'Go on – say something. Say "Don't be so clumsy, Lucy".'

'You can't help being clumsy. I don't blame you.'

'If only there were somewhere we could go. We can only understand each other with love. If you really loved me even a pile of stones would do – look at Peter Abelard.'

'Now, my dear, you're hysterical. Don't get worked up.'

'I don't have to be wound like the gramophone. I *am* worked up.'

Miles pushed the remains of lunch into the bag.

'I think we'd better go back,' he said. 'There's nothing to be gained by a scene out here.'

'It's all right, I'm not going to cry. I wasn't trying to gain anything. I just wanted to get through to you somehow, but if you are going to call me "my dear" it's hopeless, everything's utterly hopeless.'

She began to cry at once.

'You see?' Miles stood up. 'You're tired, I expect.'

She ran away up the path to hide the tears which always irritated him, but a dark snake slithered across the mud from one jungle to another and she turned back screaming.

'*Now* what is it?'

'A snake – an enormous snake.'

'Nonsense. I don't see one.'

'It's gone. It was just in front of me, about a yard away. I might have trodden on it.'

'But you didn't. It was much more frightened of you.'

'But I might have – right on it, and then I'd have been dead and it would have been quite true about no time after the present.'

'Be quiet, Lucy, it probably wasn't even poisonous.'

'Of course it was poisonous – a great slimy black snake like that.'

'Now come along, pull yourself together, and we'll go back.'

'You don't love me.'

If he loved her he would carry her home, safe from dangerous dragons.

Miles shrugged his shoulders.

'I refuse to have a scene out here, as I said before, just to pander to your over-developed sense of melodrama. You aren't in a fit state to discuss anything.'

'You don't discuss love – it just exists.'

'Come on. I've had enough.'

He walked away and she had to follow for fear of impassable horrors in the mud between them.

'Well.' With the plane behind him, so soon to take off, Miles was cheerful again. 'I think we'd better forget this whole visit.'

'Yes, Miles.'

'It wasn't a great success, was it?'

'No, Miles.'

'Better luck next time.'

'Do you think so?'

Monsoon clouds gathered in the puddle at her feet.

'Of course, bound to be disagreements, and...'

The end of the sentence was lost in the roar of the engines.

'What did you say?'

'Adjustments...' Miles shouted.

'Hadn't you better get in?'

'Perhaps I'd better. Good-bye, dear. Don't forget what I said.'

'Good-bye, Miles. I shan't forget. I promise I won't make you ashamed again.'

'That's a good girl. Don't work too hard. I think you are looking a bit under the weather.'

'A bit what?'

'Under the weather.'

'Oh...'

She stepped back, and the door between them closed.

One hot, wet week followed another. The atom-bomb exploded and the Japanese gave up fighting. Nelly had eczema and scratched on all the sitting-room chairs.

An envelope in Steve's handwriting came for Lucy from Japan. It felt so thin that she wondered if he had forgotten to enclose the letter, but when she opened it a cutting from an American forces paper fell out, a picture of Lucy on a table holding a shoe and a full glass, hair over one eye, stooping forward with a drunken leer. The heads of at least half a dozen men composed the foreground, underneath was written 'Even a limey can relax'.

Steve had added in the margin, 'Nothing to do with me, but glad to see you are enjoying yourself'. She stared at it for several minutes, turning it upside down to see if the effect was any better. It was more like an orgy with Lucy standing on her head, and on the whole less like Lucy. She could not count on Miles getting it wrong way up, he would only see it at all if someone brought it to him specially. Perhaps there were no American Forces in Southern India.

She passed the cutting over to Elizabeth.

'Does this little snap recall any happy moment for you?'

Elizabeth giggled.

'That evening was the absolute bottom. We shouldn't have thrown him out on the road, but it's like you, Lucy. It's a good likeness, though you do look sort of off your head rather.'

'That's what I thought.' Lucy folded the cutting and put it in her pocket.

Miles's next letter did not mention the photograph. He talked again of the possibility of moving to some unknown destination, then for two weeks she heard nothing. Half-way into the third week the blow fell. Miles had been shown Lucy's orgy, a direct contradiction of all she had promised him. More in sorrow and irritation than in anger, he spoke of discussing it later, of a good psychiatrist he knew who might be able to help Lucy to disembarrass herself of her aggressive exhibitionism, of the heat having gone to her head, etc., etc., and finally added in a postscript that he was flying back to England next week in an early release scheme, and thought she should make an effort to join him.

It was an effort to raise her arms to brush her hair.

'What's the matter, Lucy, do you feel ill?'

'No, thank you, Greta – at least, I don't think so. I feel very far away.'

Eleanor pressed salt tablets on her. She could not swallow her curry. A few days later she really fainted in the canteen, pulling two mugs of hot tea down on top of herself with a clatter. She came to to find Taffy and Bill fanning her with bush hats, their brown faces kind and anxious.

'Joe's gone back to your place to fetch someone.' She tried to smile.

'Funny thing, Taffy, after we pretended this happened before.'

They helped her over to a chair.

'Now keep your head down, Lucy.'

'I'm all right now, really – look.' She stood up, but the room tilted and she sat down hurriedly.

The doctor diagnosed heat exhaustion with very low blood pressure.

'She oughtn't to be here,' he told Eleanor. 'Can you fix to get her away?'

Eleanor was sure Mrs. Bannister could arrange it. Lucy lay on one side and looked out of the window and would not eat. It was all very well to talk of going away, she had too much luggage, she could never escape.

'Shall I cut your hair?' Jennifer suggested.

This seemed a good idea, but it was not worth sitting up. Jennifer worked round her head on the pillow with a pair of nail-scissors.

'It looks a bit odd,' she said at the end, but Lucy did not care, it was no longer so damp at the back of her neck. She stroked the kitten for a while, but it was too hot against her thigh, and Jennifer took it away. They all came and went.

'I'm sorry, you have to work harder,' she said, but she could not manage genuine regret.

'Don't worry about that. We've got a relief, a Burmese girl,' Eleanor told her, and Lucy was aware of a new face smiling, of Thwin in a white blouse and a long flowered skirt with a flower in the dark knot at the back of her hair.

Chapter Eighteen

They said she was better and could get up and could travel to England in the company of a nurse who was due to go home. She tried to believe them, she put her feet on the floor and then sat, waiting for something to happen, for someone to take charge. She knelt weeping into her suitcase with empty hands till Greta came and packed for her.

They travelled by sea to Calcutta, by train to Bombay, by sea from Bombay to Liverpool. Lucy shared a cabin with the nurse, but did not see her often. The nurse had a very good time on the two ships. Lucy sat in a deck-chair feeling like an old, old lady, and knowing she would never recover, but coming through the Bay of Biscay into a European November she felt a shiver of returning life. Huddled in thick sweaters and coats she stayed on the wet and plunging deck while the nurse groaned below.

'No more sunshine,' said the sailor. 'Miss it?'

'Not a bit – had enough.'

'Been out East long?'

'No, hardly any time, just over a year.'

One year and a few months, so short a visit

that some people might not notice she had gone.

'What – you back already?'

'It's not me, actually.'

'Who are you, if you aren't you?'

'I was me, but I went.'

'Went where?'

'Melted away.'

'You still look like you – only worse.'

'I can't help that. I'm so much older.'

'What, one year?'

'One lifetime.'

How many lives new and now another one, but too old, too ugly, and too ill to start explaining, arguing, pleading. She wished now she had cabled to Miles to expect her, to meet her on the cold, wet docks. But going through the Customs she was glad to be not already explaining, arguing, pleading.

She slept in the London train and arrived at Euston in a fog before she was ready. She rubbed her eyes, but the fog was still there, not yet thick, but promising a bad evening.

She telephoned first to Miles's mother.

'Hullo, is that Mrs. Spender? It's Lucy here.'

'Who?'

'Lucy – Miles's wife.'

'My dear, but how perfectly splendid. We weren't expecting you. Where are you? Come straight here.'

'I'm at Euston. Is Miles there? Could I

speak to him, please?'

'No, he's not – he's away at the moment. As a matter of fact he's gone to stay with some friends in St. John's Wood for a few nights. Wait a minute, I'll get you the address, it's on the hall table – hold on.'

Lucy hung up the receiver. There was no point in holding on for an address she knew by heart.

'It'll take me quite a while to get up to St. John's Wood this weather,' the taxi-driver told her.

'Never mind.' Perhaps she would have woken up by that time. The taxi crawled up Albany Street and along the top of Regent's Park. The Mappin Terrace and the heights of Primrose Hill were already swallowed up. From the zoo came a mournful howling to echo some far-away dream.

She tried to assemble the floating mists of her mind into an efficient framework, straightened her suit, made up her face, combed her hair smoothly back, found a dirty handkerchief in the pocket of her overcoat and thrust it to the bottom of her bag where she would be less likely to pull it out hurriedly. Her fingers closed round a key. Rachel's key, never posted, never thought of again. It lay in the palm of her hand, a little rusty.

There were no lights in the front of the house. She told the taxi-driver to wait and ran up the steps, but with her finger on the bell she hesitated. It would be interesting to see if the key still worked, fun to walk in on everyone eating in the basement and to say:

'Hullo, any tea left?'

The chairs would squeak, pushed back on the linoleum, Miles rushing forward, and Priscilla and Allan and Rachel and Henry...

'Lucy, how wonderful. Did you fly? What happened? Tell us everything. Have some toast, darling. You must be exhausted – have a chair,' and Priscilla putting on the kettle for a fresh pot as she talked.

The key turned smoothly in the lock and she stood in the dark hall and could hear nothing. The house was surely empty. She listened at the top of the basement stairs, but no china clinked, no chairs squeaked, nobody laughed. She was turning to go when she saw the line of light under the sitting-room door. The handle slipped softly under her fingers and the door opened to show her Miles and Rachel on the big divan, deeply involved. They both sat up as she gasped.

'Why, Lucy' Rachel cried, holding out her hands automatically welcoming. 'Have you had tea?'

Miles said: 'Oh, damn.'

She did not bang the door, she left as quietly as she had come, as if thoughtful for a sleeping child or the obsequies of a dead love. She laid the key on the hall table. Out on the step she blinked. It was still not quite dark; her eyes were clouded with Rachel's shimmering, sharp yellow housecoat.

'Take it in, lady?' The taxi-driver indicated her luggage.

'Not yet, I'm afraid. They're all away.'

'Where now?'

'Kensington – I'm so sorry.'

'That's all right, lady, you pay.'

She gave him Mrs. Spender's address. There she could at least get rid of her things – and then what? Perhaps even stay the night, since Miles was elsewhere. She did not feel anything. She pushed her hands deep into her pockets and her chin into her collar. Crossing Hyde Park they were caught up in the rush hour, intensified by fog.

'Seen the clock lately?' the driver asked when he drew up outside Mrs. Spender's block of flats.

'It's all right,' Lucy assured him. 'Would you just wait again while I go up and see if they are in?'

There was a lift to the fourth floor. Mrs. Spender was at home in powder blue and pearls, and once Lucy had introduced herself, delighted to see her.

'My dear, come into the warm, you're shivering. Let me look at you. Have you had tea? Where are your things?'

As Lucy was going out of the door to settle

with the taxi, Mrs. Spender followed her into the passage with a letter.

'My dear, I was going to tell you about this when you rang from the station, but we were cut off. The young man called yesterday.'

Going down in the lift she read:

'Lucy dear. So sorry to miss you all over the world. Tried in Rangoon but as you had gone I thought you would be home before me. I leave for Dublin tomorrow night. It would have been a pleasure to see you and make sure you have really recovered. I may be in England again next spring.

'Love, Steve.'

'Still nobody home?' asked the taxi-driver. 'Aren't you the prodigal daughter?'

Lucy told him, without hope, that she was now suddenly in a tearing hurry. She named Steve's West End hotel. The driver was dubious.

'Wouldn't get there in a hurry any night at this time, let alone with this blooming fog on top.'

'Please try.'

'I'll try all right.'

This time she sat on the edge of the seat, pushing the taxi forward with every bone in her body. The hands in her pockets were clenched and clammy.

At the hotel she ran up the steps two at a

time, crashed through the swing doors and reached the reception desk breathless.

'Mr. McMahon, please.'

'McMahon – let me see now. He's checked out.'

'How long ago?'

With maddening deliberation the receptionist considered the clock.

'Can't have been more than twenty minutes, more like fifteen.'

'Did he leave any address?'

'No – just care of his paper in the book.'

'Could you tell me the night trains to Dublin, please?'

'To Dublin – now let me see. Where do you want to go from, Fishguard or Liverpool?'

He pulled out ABC's and Bradshaws from under the desk and began to thumb the pages muttering. In five minutes he had established that the night train from Paddington left much later than the one from Euston.

'Doubt if you'd catch the Euston train now,' he added, but Lucy was already out of earshot.

'Euston,' she panted to the taxi-driver.

'This is where we came in,' he said. 'It'll be like home to see it again.'

'Dublin?' the porter queried. 'Doubt if you'll make it now, with all this stuff.'

'Keep the luggage till I get back then.' She began to run, stopping only for a platform ticket to take her past the barrier. The guard was going down the train slamming the doors.

'Hurry up there – in you get.'

She was pulled up and stood leaning against the corridor to get her breath back. The train steamed out. Goodbye, Euston, good-bye, Miles, good-bye, Steve, who was probably travelling via Fishguard. The taxi-driver had all her money, the porter all her luggage. She began to laugh, leaning her head on the bar of the window, shaking silently.

'Laughing or crying?' Steve asked, his arm round her shoulders.

'How did you know I was here?'

'Watched your gallant arrival, never thought you'd make it.'

'I was just laughing because I thought you might have gone from Paddington. I haven't any money and only a platform ticket. Have you got a seat?'

'A whole empty carriage – first class. Come along.'

He led her up the train.

She sat down nervously opposite him wondering what she had done. He did not touch her again.

'Are you better, Lucy?'

'Yes, thank you. Are you all right?'

'Yes, thank you. When did you get back to London?'

'Ages ago – about three o'clock.'

'This afternoon?'

'Yes.'

'And now you are going abroad again?'

'I suppose so.'

'Quite right – mustn't get in a rut.'

'Oh, Steve, you're laughing at me.'

'Darling, what else can I do? You're so sweet. Now tell me what happened during your visit to England.'

'Miles doesn't love me.'

'I know that.'

'How?'

'I've seen you together – it stood out a mile. Sorry, not meaning to be funny.'

He was still very brown, but thinner.

'You haven't been ill, Steve?'

'No, that was you – if you remember.'

'You aren't helping.'

'Then you can't say afterwards I influenced you. Are you running away from, or to?'

'How do you mean?'

'From Miles, or to me?'

'How can you still ask?'

'For the pleasure of hearing you say it.'

'Then I shan't, but whatever happens, whether you want me or not, I shall still have to borrow an awful lot of money off you.'

'You could get out at the next stop and walk back,' Steve said, holding out his arms.

The publishers hope that this book has given you enjoyable reading. Large Print Books are especially designed to be as easy to see and hold as possible. If you wish a complete list of our books please ask at your local library or write directly to:

Magna Large Print Books
Magna House, Long Preston,
Skipton, North Yorkshire.
BD23 4ND

This Large Print Book, for people
who cannot read normal print,
is published under the auspices of

THE ULVERSCROFT FOUNDATION